D0530572

NO GOLD FOR TINA

Newspaper reporter Desmond Tearle, investigating the murder of racketeer Daks Hale, finds that the principal suspect has been framed. Then he discovers that Hale's mistress, the deadly Tina Tallan, had arranged the murder and intends to take over Hale's gang. Tearle, the object of her desire, becomes embroiled in Tina's world, as he assists her in a bank robbery. And when the robbery goes wrong, the bodies begin to pile up, with Tearle himself earmarked for a cruel death . . .

Books by John Robb
in the Linford Mystery Library:

JAILBREAK

JOHN ROBB

NO GOLD FOR TINA

Complete and Unabridged

LINFORD
Leicester

First published in Great Britain

First Linford Edition
published 2011

British Library CIP Data

Robb, John.
  No gold for Tina. - -
  (Linford mystery library)
  1. Journalists- -Fiction. 2. Gangsters- -Crimes
against- -Fiction. 3. Murder- -Investigation- -
Fiction. 4. Detective and mystery stories.
  5. Large type books.
  I. Title II. Series
  823.9'14–dc22

  ISBN 978–1–44480–609–0

Published by
F. A. Thorpe (Publishing)
Anstey, Leicestershire

Set by Words & Graphics Ltd.
Anstey, Leicestershire
Printed and bound in Great Britain by
T. J. International Ltd., Padstow, Cornwall

This book is printed on acid-free paper

1

A Hick With A Roll

Suzette watched the young hick who sat on the bar stool trying to look like he was used to this sort of thing. But he wasn't kidding Suzette any. Nothing much ever kidded Suzette. She'd seen it all before. And she'd never been impressed. She'd even seen this type before — the type with adolescent pimples and a fat roll of folding money. But not so often. Nice and easy game like this doesn't offer itself to a gal every day.

Suzette leaned towards the hick.

She said: 'I'm Suzette. Ain't seen you around before, stranger.'

He didn't answer. He didn't even look at her. He fixed his frightened eyes on the rows of bottles.

Then his blotched pan turned scarlet. But he was trying to look cold. Look tough.

He was still not looking at her when he said: 'Hiyer, Suzette. I'm Dick Farrel. I haven't noticed you either.'

It didn't sound so good. That line just wasn't convincing at all. But Suzette didn't let him know that. A girl has to play these suckers up big. Then they fall.

'I haven't seen you either,' she told him. 'But Vallis City sure is a big place. Still . . .'

She switched an appreciative glance at him. The shoulders were narrow and didn't provide any inspiration. But she wasn't letting him think that. Not while he had a big roll of bucks tucked away.

The question came in just the way she'd expected.

'How's about having a drink, Suzette?'

'Sure. I'll take a deep rye with Angostura. You oughta try that, too. It's a whole lot better than that canned beer you're drinking.'

The barman was already pouring. Suzette took hers over a single breath. Then she smiled at the hick.

It's hard to look tough when you're young. When you're green.

Things can happen to a guy in a big city. Things you only read about back in the hometown with its one main street, a general trading store and a sheriff's office. Women, for instance. They weren't so bashful here. Like Suzette. Of course, Suzette might like the sight of that fat roll of dough he had. But not necessarily . . .

There was that gal he met yesterday. He hadn't had more than a couple of bucks when he met up with her. Right then, he'd been looking for a job. Trying to make good. But she'd taken up with him. And she'd been no ordinary gal.

She'd scared him a bit at first — even more than Suzette was doing. But she was different to Suzette. More polished. Taken him to her home. It was a pity about her husband coming right back. Not that he'd seen the husband. But she'd heard him. He'd had to beat it quick. Had to jump clear over a wall then run like hell from a suspicious cop. And later he'd found she'd put this fat load of bucks in his pocket.

Farrel figured that maybe there was something about him. Maybe he had that sort of personality.

Suzette cut in on his thoughts. She said: 'There's only one way to take this poison — fast and smooth. But I guess you'll know all about that.'

He gave her a weak grin and nodded. Yeah, he said, he knew all about that.

He got it down nearly as fast as Suzette. And he didn't cough a lot, either.

'We could both use another,' Suzette suggested.

When the glasses were empty for the second time, the sucker was near to being ready. There was a blank and flat look about his eyes and he was swaying a bit on the stool. A couple more at the apartment and he'd be in fine condition.

'I gotta go home,' she told him. Her voice was on velvet. 'I'm kinda expecting a long-distance phone call. It ain't too important, but I said I'd be there. But that's no reason for me to go alone.'

'Sure thing ... that's a swell idea. Suzette. Let's go ... '

They went.

Her apartment was only a couple of blocks off. They walked the distance and he was still swaying as they thrust through the night crowds.

The elevator didn't stop until they were at the top — and that was fifteen floors up.

It's a funny thing about apartment blocks, but the higher up you get the lower is your dignity. Even the street-level lettings in this place weren't exactly salubrious. They went for eighteen bucks a week. Suzette paid a quarter of that amount, and she was overcharged. But that didn't worry her any.

She opened the door and they entered a small sitting room. Farrel blinked at a stained carpet, at a few gilded and sagging chairs, at the framed portraits that were hung on the walls.

Suzette went to a table. She poured a couple of drinks. The hick wasn't watching her while she did it. But even if he had watched, he wouldn't have seen her drop a pink tablet into one of the glasses. Suzette handled these situations the smart way.

She told him: 'This is rum. It makes a nice change.'

He'd got the idea now. He didn't cough even once and he figured he sounded tough as he handed the empty glass to her and said: 'I could use that again.'

Suzette gave him another. He wanted to take this one fast, too. But somehow it didn't work out that way. His hands felt heavy so it was hard work getting the liquor to his lips.

Some of the stuff dribbled down his chin and on to his collar.

He said: 'I guess I'll take it easy, Suzette . . . '

And he swayed towards one of the chairs.

But he didn't reach the chair. He was almost in reach of it when he flopped to the carpet. And there he stayed, his mouth pressed against the gritty pile of the carpet.

Suzette stood over him, giving a long look. She turned him over with the toe of a satin evening shoe. For a short while she regarded the face critically. Then she laughed and crossed to the phone.

When a voice came through she said: 'Say, Sprots, you'd better come over here.

I want you to help me get rid of a guy. He's on the carpet right now and it makes the place look kinda untidy.'

The voice at the other end said: 'So you've met up with it soft, eh Suzette? What's he worth to you?'

'A couple of hundred bucks, maybe. It's not a lot, but I guess it was worth it because he's safe. He's so young and so dumb you can almost smell the talcum.'

Sprots told her he'd be right over.

Then Suzette hitched up her long skirt and bent over Farrel. She groped in the pockets of his pants and hauled out a thick wad of paper. She flicked through it like it was a pack of cards.

She said to herself in a gentle way: 'Nine hundred and forty. Not bad. This bum musta had a legacy or something.'

Very carefully, Suzette detached five twenty-dollar bills and put them on the table. The rest she pushed behind one of the wall pictures. Suzette liked the details to be right.

Then she finished her drink.

It was ten minutes later that Sprots arrived. Sprots did not need to push the door buzz. He had a key and he used it. He stood just inside the room, watching the man on the floor. A dead cigar was inserted between his thick lips and he rolled it from corner to corner.

He said: 'Jeeze, he's only a kid. You must be operating in a nursery these days.'

'Could be,' Suzette told him. 'I've always liked to think of the future.'

Ten years before, Sprots had been in the prize ring. But he hadn't made a career out of that. Not after he'd been belted to sleep by a heavy from Charleston. After that Sprots had decided that fighting with gloves on just wasn't his vocation. That was the way with him. Yellow.

But he still had the build that goes with a good fighter. Two hundred pounds of hard cased muscle, most of it around the shoulders and arms. And he had looks, too. Corrugated black hair and a big, olive tinted pan. The sort of good looks that makes nice girls shudder and try to remember what their old mom told them.

Right now, Sprots gave up his distant inspection and checked over the sucker's pockets.

He extracted some papers, a folded magazine, but no dough.

'This bum's from a place by name of Rich Valley,' he said, looking at a letter. 'His name's Richard Farrel, too. But that don't interest me so much. How much did he carry and what's my cut out of it?'

Suzette gave herself a cigarette before answering. Then she said: 'It's on the table — all of it. It's around a century, like I thought. You get him outa here and we split two ways.'

Sprots seemed undecided. He knew quite well that the kid must have been padded with a whole lot more than Suzette had admitted. But there wasn't a lot he could do about it. And fifty bucks was a nice pick up just for carrying him down the back stairs and leaving him in one of the quiet back streets. When he recovered, the chances were he'd never have the nerve to go to the cops. But even if he did, no one could prove a thing. Suzette could organise a sweet roll when the right prospect came along. And this kid was one of the best prospects he'd seen. Young and pure. Too scared, most likely, to make trouble. 'Okay,' Sprots said. 'Gimme my cut and I'll move the baggage.'

Suzette split the bills and gave him half.

Then the phone bell started ringing.

'Expecting someone?' Sprots asked, pushing his hat back from his forehead.

Suzette said she wasn't.

It was Tickie at the other end — the barman at the joint where she'd met up with Farrel. And Tickie sounded like something was on his mind.

'Say, Suzette, I thought maybe I'd better ring you because this is urgent,' he said. 'Have you still got that guy with you that you took out of here?'

Suzette wasn't giving.

'He could have gone. But what's the interest?'

'There's plenty of interest. The cops have just been in my bar asking for a guy who could be him. And right now they're on their way to your apartment. I had to help them because that guy's dangerous. He's wanted for a killing.'

2

A Call To Cullen

Suzette didn't allow herself time to be surprised. And that says a whole lot for her willpower. Most girls would have spent some time wondering how it was that this pimpled hick could get around to murder. But Suzette wasn't made that way. She'd play her guessing games later. Right now, there was no more than a couple of minutes to spare.

She told Sprots what Tickie had said. Sprots didn't like it any. But Suzette was giving the orders.

'Get him out,' she said. 'If he's found doped in here we'll both go into retirement for a long time. Even if he is a killer, the cops'll still use a case like that against us. Get him out, then keep away. And remember — you've never been near this place tonight.'

Sprots was sweating when he raised the

kid on to his shoulders. It wasn't the sweat of physical work. He could handle that side of it okay. It was the sweat of fear. Suzette checked that the corridor was clear, and he ran towards the back staircase.

When Sprots had gone, Suzette picked the glass from the carpet and rubbed in the moisture with her foot. That was all she had time to do before the law arrived.

A cop with a pink face and a belly that drooped and swayed pushed into the apartment. Suzette recognised him.

She'd seen him around this precinct often enough. This was Captain Cullen of the Homicide Bureau. And Cullen was said to be plenty smart. Maybe too smart. Behind Cullen were three uniformed cops.

Cullen stopped in the middle of the room and looked around. He looked slowly, absorbing every detail. Then he asked: 'You Suzette Dailey?'

She was trying to look puzzled.

'That's what I've always thought. But what do you boys want? I've never had trouble with the cops . . . '

Cullen wasn't letting that one pass.

'You're having trouble right now — unless you get around to some cooperation. Where's your boy friend — the one you dazzled out of the bar about an hour ago?'

Suzette sat on the arm of a chair. She decided to play this the safe way. To keep as near to the facts as she could.

'He must've left twenty minutes back. But why do you wanta know?'

Cullen ignored the question.

'Did he say where he was going?'

'No. I guess he'd lost interest in me.'

Cullen was standing beside the table. He picked up a letter. The letter that had been in Farrel's pocket. The one that Sprots had been looking at. Sprots was careless. He left things around.

Cullen spent quite a time looking at the envelope. Then he pulled out a single folded sheet of notepaper and read it. His mouth framed some of the words. When he'd done that he pushed the lot into a pocket and took a steady look at Suzette.

'Do your friends always leave their letters with you?'

13

Suzette was getting scared — really scared. There was a desperate intensity about her voice.

'Gee . . . I guess it musta fallen out of his suit.'

'Yeah. And it could have been taken out of his suit. Taken with some other things. That bum was carrying a lot of dough. Or didn't you know that?'

She was lighting another cigarette. Her hand wasn't so steady. 'I didn't know.'

Cullen paced slowly towards her. The side of his palm flashed up and knocked the cigarette from her lips. Then he pointed to the wet patch on the carpet.

'Someone spilled a drink in here, too. And it wasn't long ago. The carpet's still damp. How did that happen?'

'I — I dropped my glass when he grabbed me . . . that's all, captain.'

Cullen scratched his bristly grey hair. Then he looked at the uniformed officers while jerking his thumb towards Suzette.

'Take her in. I ain't satisfied with this doll.'

Suzette swore. Not loud and not for very long. But the four words she used made even the law regard her with a mixture of surprise and admiration. Not many girls knew those kind of words.

* * *

Desmond Tearle was sleeping behind his desk in the newsroom of the *Morning Tribune*. One elbow was flopped on the keys of his typewriter and his chin rested on a pad of copy paper. He was used to relaxing in that way, particularly at around midnight when the main edition is rolling off the presses. It was midnight right now. If everything went according to plan he'd stay like this for another hour and then fade discreetly out of the office, continuing his rest in his bed.

But everything did not go according to plan. He was wakened by a slap across the back of his neck that felt like the fall of an axe. The hand belonged to Hyman, the city editor.

Hyman said: 'Get on your feet and get moving. I wantya to see Cullen. It seems he's pulled in some girl who may have a lead on the Hale killing.'

Tearle massaged his eyes and gave it to Hyman sour.

'What's the fuss? That guy was murdered nearly twenty-four hours ago and since then we've had more than fifty leads on the story and none of them any good. I figure this'll be the same. Can't you let a reporter rest?'

Hyman didn't look pleased. He rubbed a hand through his thin hair and glared back at Tearle. He was thinking that the trouble with Tearle was that he was a good reporter when he was interested. But he couldn't remember when he'd last been interested.

'You'll get down to the station and see Cullen. I just got this tip-off a minute ago and I'm not risking passing it up. It could be hot.'

Tearle was thinking that Hyman wasn't such a bad city editor. His only fault was that he insisted on building his reputation through other guys' work.

'Okay,' he said. 'I guess I gotta go. But after I've seen Cullen I'm moving straight on to my apartment. I'm a weary man.'

He straightened his hat, eased up his

16

necktie, and wondered what the hell a girl could have to do with the killing of a big shot racketeer like Daks Hale.

Daks had been found that morning with a single slug embedded in his head. It must have been a peaceful kind of end because it had happened while he was in bed. The clothes were not disturbed. Almost humane. Better than a punk like Daks had deserved.

Tearle climbed into his coupé and headed towards the station.

★ ★ ★

Cullen liked to think he was tough. He liked to administer the law the rough way. And he liked to let everyone know about it. He figured that the only good folks are scared folks. When Tearle eased into his office, Cullen was working on Suzette.

But this was only a preliminary workout. Nothing too drastic yet. Suzette was hunched in a deep leather chair. The treatment consisted of Cullen asking questions.

Up to now she hadn't been giving the

answers he wanted.

He paused as Tearle stood inside the doorway. Then he nodded to a uniformed cop who was lounging against a wall.

'Take her away,' he told him. 'I'll be talking to her again later.'

Tearle watched while Suzette was helped out of the office, That girl wasn't looking so good. She was scared and she was hurt.

'Did she slay Daks?'

Cullen grinned. It was a tired grin.

'Hell, no. But she's been with the guy who did. If she'd tell us what she knows about him we might let her go. But she won't.'

'You've been moving fast. Who did the job and what put you on to him?'

Cullen paused to light a short stemmed and strong smelling pipe. It was burning nicely when he said: 'A patrolman saw a guy leaving Dak's place at about the time of the killing. He was jumping over the wall. This cop thought maybe it was just another tramp. but he gives chase. This guy gets away but we got a good description. He was mighty tender for that kinda work. No more than twenty-two or three. We didn't want to scare him out of town, so we decided not to say anything to you boys.'

'Then you traced him to this dame. What's her name?'

'It could be anything, but for business purposes she calls herself Suzette Simone.'

Tearle said: 'It seems kinda hard on the dame. She may not know anything about this guy. He needn't have stayed long enough to give her his life history.'

Cullen bit on the stem of his pipe. Then he looked down at his belly.

He told Tearle about the letter.

'I figure that she picked that bum up because he was carrying plenty of dough — Dak's dough that he got from his room when he killed him. Dak's clothes had been frisked when we arrived and there wasn't a cent in his pockets. Then I figure she slipped him a Mickey Finn. One of her boy friends would get him out. Suzette has played that way before.'

Cullen paused. Then he added: 'She ain't carrying the dough, but right now I've got some of my boys on the job of taking her apartment to pieces. I figure we'll find it there. And we'll find this guy, too. They'll have stuck him up some side street. I'm having those combed . . . but if Suzette'd talk we find him just that much faster.'

Tearle made a few notes on a scrap of paper from Cullen's desk. He wasn't so convinced about that kid Farrel. A whole lot of facts didn't seem to fit in with him as a killer. But it all looked like building into a nice news story. Pity it was too late for the big edition.

'Mind if I put this over to my office?' he asked.

Cullen said he didn't mind. As Tearle put his hand on the phone the bell inside it started to ring. Without thinking much about it, he put the receiver to his ear.

A woman's voice came through. It was a rich and soft sort of voice. And it had a very faint accent that could have been French or Spanish.

It said: 'Don't worry about the girl. The set-up looks okay now. She can go, but . . .'

And that was all it said. Anyway, all that

Tearle heard. Cullen pulled the instrument out of his hand. He covered the mouthpiece for a second as he hissed: 'Newsboys may be goddammed important, but they don't take the calls in my office.'

Then he took up the conversation. Not that he took much part in it. Not beyond saying 'yeah' occasionally. Tearle watched him. He was getting curious.

Somehow, that woman's voice was familiar. But he couldn't place it. Not yet, anyway, but he knew he'd heard it before. And the words she had used were kind of curious, also.

'*Don't worry about the girl. The set-up looks okay now. She can go . . .* ' That sounded like an order. And it could apply to Suzette.

A man in a stained and crumpled suit came in the office just before Cullen had finished talking. A man with cold, flat eyes which never blinked. He turned them on Tearle for a few moments. Tearle looked right back. This was Lieutenant Bakana. He knew Bakana. Bakana was a cop who didn't like the newspapers. The regard was mutual.

When Cullen had slammed down the phone, Bakana said to him: 'We've found that guy Farrel. He was doped but he's okay now. Do you want him in?'

Cullen nodded.

'Yeah, do that. And Suzette . . . she can go. We won't be needing her.'

Bakana stroked his thin chin.

'She had his dough. I was gonna tell you we found that in her apartment.'

'Maybe, but that doesn't matter any.'

Bakana was beginning to look surprised.

'But that's an offence that can carry from one to fifteen years.'

Cullen slapped his belly. It quivered. He had a habit of doing that when he wasn't pleased.

'I don't need legal tuition. I said let her go and that's just what I mean.'

Bakana opened his face as if he was going to say more. Then he changed his mind, and went out. He made a lot of noise closing the door.

Tearle sat himself in a deep chair. He didn't feel like sleep any more. But he'd have liked a drink. A long bourbon. He promised himself one — or maybe more than one — just as soon as it could be fixed. But right now there was something else on his mind that had to take precedence.

'So you're gonna hold this kid Farrel for the killing of Daks?'

Cullen was relighting his pipe. He nodded.

'Sure. What do you expect me to do? Put him up in a civic parade?'

Tearle's brain was working fast. It was collating and examining facts.

He said: 'You must be kidding. That guy never slew Daks.'

Cullen eased into the swivel chair behind his desk. It creaked under the tonnage.

'Yeah? That's what you think. But you don't know it all.'

'I know what you've told me, and it doesn't add up to murder. Would a guy who'd put a slug into Daks and taken his roll hang around town all the next day spending the dough?'

Tearle was watching Cullen. But the cop just gave a fat grin.

'I guess he must be dumb. He musta broken into that house to see what he could find. Maybe he didn't know it was Daks Hale's home, or he'd have tried somewhere else. I figure he got into Daks' room, was disturbed and fired because he was scared.'

It's hard work pedalling a phony story to a good reporter. Tearle grinned back.

'Then he wasn't just dumb — he was crazy. You want me to believe that Farrel was disturbed by someone outside the room and shot Daks dead because of it!'

'I didn't say anything about someone outside the room. I figure that Daks himself woke up.'

Tearle sighed. It was a loud and obvious sigh.

'Yet your own official reports given out twelve hours back said that Daks had been shot while he slept. The bedclothes weren't even disturbed.'

Cullen had been talked into a tight place. There was a curious look about him as he stared at Tearle. Half fright. Half something a whole lot worse than fright.

He said: 'Okay . . . so all the details don't fit. But they will later. Just a few days'll fix that.'

Tearle had stopped grinning as he said: 'A murder indictment has to be served from the district attorney's office. It's a public prosecution. You can't do it. And the D.A. will have you fired if you go to him with that kind of evidence.'

Suddenly a shake came into Cullen's voice. The shake of a man who's trying to fight down a hot surge of fury.

'The murder charge'll come when the evidence is complete. Until then I'll hold him as a material witness. I don't need the D.A.'s permit to do that.'

Tearle uncoiled his long length from the chair. He moved towards the desk and leaned over it. His bunched fist waved near Cullen's pan.

'You mean you'll hold him until you've cooked enough evidence to frame him into an electric chair . . . yeah, that's what I said . . . frame him. You've fixed other poor bums that way before, but not for anything like a killing. I don't know what stakes your playing for, but . . . '

The door opened and Lieutenant Bakana pushed a thin and trembling kid into the room. A kid whose face was as white as milk and whose mouth hung slack. His eyes were floating in moisture.

It was Farrel.

3

Tina

Tearle knew just what was going to happen. He wanted to stay in that office so that he could see it happen. He wanted his opinion of Farrel confirmed. An opinion that this kid hadn't the nerve to slay a gnat. But Cullen wasn't thinking along those lines.

'We're gonna have an official interrogation,' he rasped. 'We don't have the newspapers in on those.'

Tearle stayed still.

'You'll be working towards getting a signed statement from this kid?' he said softly.

Cullen nodded. That was what they were aiming at, he said.

Tearle glanced at Farrel. His wrists were linked by glittering handcuffs. But that wasn't enough. Bakana had a grip on the back of his collar. He was twisting it tight so that the kid had trouble in

27

drawing his sobbing breath.

Tearle said: 'It shouldn't take you long. Ten minutes with your boys and he'll sign anything.'

He moved towards the door. On the way be stopped beside Bakana. He looked at the cop's fists gripping the collar.

'You must be awful scared to take that sort of precaution,' he breathed. Then he eased out of the office.

It was at the moment that he slumped into his seat in the coupé that he remembered something. Something that his subconscious mind had been groping for during the past ten minutes.

He remembered that girl who had spoken on Cullen's phone The recognition exploded so suddenly and vividly that be cursed himself for not being able to place her immediately. But that was the way it went when it came to trying to recognise voices. The more obvious they were the longer it took.

He glanced at his strap watch. Fifteen minutes past two. The time couldn't be better. It would have that nice element of surprise. But maybe the drink would have to wait.

It was a fast drive to the outskirts of the city. It ended when he reached an avenue of large houses, each in its own grounds. This was where the boys who had made good lived. It was where the racketeer Daks Hale had lived until a slug had put an end to him.

Tearle knew the house. It was approached by a wide and curving drive. But he did not take his coupé up there. He wanted nothing to spoil this surprise. He left the car on the road.

Lights showed through the ground floor windows. For a home in mourning, this was kind of unusual. Tearle turned the handle on the big double door. That was locked. He pressed the bell.

It was quite a time before the door was opened. And when it did a man in a dinner suit stood opposite him. A man who was well past six feet tall and whose pan looked like it had been hammered into shape by some amateur sculptor. And the amateur hadn't made such a good job of it.

Tearle grinned at him.

He said: 'Hiyer, Ivan. I guess you've

just had a big day.'

That was a safe bet. Ivan Rasewitz had been a big guy in Daks' mob. And that wasn't just referring to his physique. Ivan had been a useful triggerman. If he'd always done his social duty, Ivan would have spent a lot of dough on wreaths. There were quite a few folks in the city cemetery who'd seen Ivan just before they died.

Tearle was still standing in the outside darkness.

Ivan said: 'Who the hell is it?'

Tearle didn't keep him guessing. He pushed into the hall. The two were about of a size and they stood close, facing each other. Ivan didn't seem so pleased.

'Say, you're that newspaper guy. What'yer want here? We've got nothin' to say. The cops'll tell you all you want to know.'

'Yeah. That's one thing about the cops — they'll always tell us everything we want to know, so long as we don't want to know too much. But I didn't come here to yap with you. Tell Tina I'd like to see her.'

Ivan's slit eyes narrowed still further.

'Say, you must think you're pretty

smart coming here and asking for Miss Tallan at this time. Right now she's asleep and that's what you'll be doing unless you get right out . . . '

Ivan bunched his mitts. They were as large as a bunch of bananas. But they didn't impress Tearle any. He wasn't fragile, either.

'Do you tell her, or do I have to find her myself?'

There was no need for Ivan to answer the question. A woman's voice did it for him.

It said: 'So it's a reporter . . . Mister Tearle. Come right in.'

It was the faint foreign accent. Velvety. And its owner was velvety, too.

She was standing in the middle of the hall. And even the way she stood was unusual. One length of leg was a bit in front of the other and it showed through the side slit in her white brocade evening dress. A hand with long fingers rested on her waist. The other hand held a cigarette in a holder.

Tearle had a long gander at her. It would have been wrong to have rushed that. Tina was worth careful inspection.

31

She said: 'Take your time, but you'd be more comfortable in the lounge.'

Tearle met her eyes. He'd seen Tina before. But she'd never looked like this. A nice looker, sure, and maybe a bit more intelligent than most. But still just a mobster's girl.

Now she was different. In her rich and slightly parted lips, in her raven hair, in her deep and dark eyes, in all her features there was an insidious suggestion of strength. Yes, that was it — strength. And confidence, too. There was even a lurking air of amusement about her as she looked at Tearle.

Tearle said: 'It doesn't look like you're exactly in mourning for your boy friend.'

She pushed smoke down her nostrils.

'I ain't. Right now Daks won't be worrying, so I ain't worrying either.'

She said it casually. Usually it was tough when a woman like her lost her man. Men like Daks were pearls and oysters to girls like Tina. And the supply of both was apt to end if a bereavement intervened. But Tina wasn't acting as if she was faced with such a calamity.

32

Tearle said: 'I wanta talk to you, Tina . . . and I want to do it alone.'

'Sure, you can talk to me. But I guess Ivan'll hang around. I'm relying on Ivan now that Daks has gone.'

She turned and moved into the room. Tearle followed with Ivan right behind him. He didn't want Ivan there, but he figured there was nothing he could do about it.

That room was like the rest of the house. It was typical of a high-class hoodlum's idea of luxury living. Early Virginian period furniture was mixed with chromium tubed chairs and concealed lighting. And there was a cute silver statue of Cupid wrestling with a woman called Temptation. The room was comfortable enough, but it looked like the result of an earthquake in a department store.

Tina stood with her back to the fireplace — a streamlined electric fire set in an expensive brick hearth. She watched Tearle as he glanced around.

'I'm getting most of this junk sorted out,' she told him. 'This was the way Daks liked it. But I've got other ideas.'

'So you're figuring on staying on in this house.'

She nodded.

'Why not. It's the natural thing to do and I'm all in favour of letting nature have its way.'

Tearle said: 'I thought maybe Daks' mob would have some sort of interest in his property. I guess those boys'll be breaking up now. Don't they want a share-out first? Or are they letting you have this estate as your cut?'

That look of amusement was still there when she answered.

'The boys aren't breaking up. And I don't like you to talk about them as a mob, Mister Tearle. They are business associates, you see?'

Tearle said quietly that he saw.

Then he said: 'And who's gonna run the . . . business?'

'I am.'

It came out just like that. Indifferently and with a slight gesture of the cigarette holder. Tearle groped for his own cigarettes. He felt he needed a smoke. And a drink, too. It was like Tina could

34

read his thoughts. She moved over to a cocktail cabinet and poured him a whisky. A big measure of scotch. Not the kind of whisky he usually took, but Tearle wasn't in a mood to worry about that. He drank it fast.

His tired brain was humming. Daks' mob had been up to the eyebrows in every honky racket in the city. It had been figured that protection money paid to city cops and officials ran into five thousand bucks a week.

And this was what the ex-mobster's girl was planning to take over.

'You're crazy. Dames don't operate these rackets. Daks had a tough mob. Yeah . . . I said mob.'

She switched her glance to Ivan.

'Show that news bum who gives the orders around here. Put him outa this house. And do it the hard way.'

Ivan had been sitting on the arm of a chair. Tearle watched him get slowly to his feet. It was like the formation of a mountain. He said: 'Sure thing. Tina.' Then Tearle saw him move forward.

But Ivan wasn't taking any chances. He

pushed his right hand into his jacket pocket and when he pulled it out four of his fingers were encircled by bands of brass. In this kind of work he figured that a knuckleduster was a help.

Tearle thought: 'Hell . . . this isn't what I came here for.'

And that was exactly right. No guy goes visiting in the hope of being slugged with a knuckleduster. But right now, he didn't want any sort of violence. He just wanted to talk with Tina. There was that phone call she made to Cullen. He wanted to uncover something about that.

But there is some trouble that just can't be sidestepped. There are times in every man's existence when diplomacy doesn't work any more. When you've got to be primitive. Got to rely on speed and muscle. Tearle figured that this was one of those times.

Right behind them there was one of those small round occasional tables. The sort that can be held easily in one hand. That was where the silver statue stood: Cupid and the woman labelled tempta-tion. Tearle grabbed it. It was badly balanced as a throwing article. But he took a chance. He hurled it towards Ivan's head. It missed by a foot and smashed against the far wall.

Ivan was almost in reach of him. His right hand was slightly extended and moving up and down like a pugilist searching for an opening. Tearle didn't intend him to find an opening. Even a light touch with that armoured mitt would be enough to splinter a bone. And Ivan didn't look like he'd worry about a detail such as a damaged bone.

Still easing back, Tearle picked up the table, holding it by two of its legs.

Even this wasn't a perfect weapon. No man can move fast with even a light table in his hands. But it was a hell of a lot better than nothing.

Ivan stopped. He was breathing heavily and making a lot of noise while doing it. Like a gorilla surveying a distant slab of meat. But he wasn't going in for that meat yet. Not until Tearle had taken a swing with the table and missed. Then he'd move in.

Ivan started to circle round Tearle. And

Tearle moved with him.

Tearle rasped: 'I thought you were told to put me out the hard way. What'yer scared of? Tina wasn't counting on seeing a dancing show from her tough canary.'

It had just the effect that Tearle had wanted. Ivan was the sort of man who hasn't a lot of brain, but has plenty of emotion. He stopped his circling movement for just long enough for him to figure out that a canary was yellow. Then he gave a single oath and rushed in.

It was a weaving rush and the top of the table he was holding made it difficult for Tearle to follow his exact movements. That was why his sideways swing missed Ivan's head. But the wood hit one of his elbows. Ivan swore again and spun round under the force of the blow. His face was twisted with pain. The elbow is a sensitive part of the anatomy.

But Tearle wasn't thinking about Ivan's sufferings. He was concerned with a little matter of self-preservation. And he figured that the best way of looking after himself was to fix this monkey so he'd be out of circulation for a few minutes. He raised the table again. This time, he didn't intend to miss the top of Ivan's cropped skull.

And he didn't.

Ivan made an attempt to sidestep, but it was too late. The edge of wood contacted thick bone. Ivan folded on to the carpet as though he'd suddenly decided to take a rest. He stayed there motionless, his face turned up towards the ceiling.

Tearle dropped the table. He dropped it on to Ivan's pan. Then he faced Tina.

Tina was standing in just the same position as she'd been in when she'd given the order to Ivan.

She was still in front of that fireplace. And she still looked relaxed. She looked first at Ivan then at Tearle. Her lips were curved in the hint of a smile.

After a while she said: 'You've got a way of getting things done and I like it . . . hard and rough. Not many guys can put Ivan to sleep.'

Tearle was still breathing hard after his exertions.

'You can save that, sister,' he told her. 'I came here for a nice quiet talk with you and that's still what I aim to have.'

She sat herself in a deep chair.

'Okay. I'm the sociable kind. Fix yourself with another drink then start talking.'

He poured himself the drink. He found a bottle of bourbon and put a lot of that in the tumbler. His breath started to come easier after the first pull.

He was watching Tina carefully when he said: 'Why did you tell Cullen to let Suzette go?'

It had its effect. Tina raised her pencilled eyebrows. She wasn't smiling now. And Tearle found her oval eyes fixed right on him.

She said in an oddly even sort of voice: 'You're asking an interesting kinda question. But before I try giving any answers I'd like to get some facts right. What gave you the idea I give orders to the police chief and who the hell's Suzette?'

Tearle finished the bourbon. He walked to the cabinet and gave himself another. He sensed that eyes were on him as he dispensed the drink.

'I was in Cullen's office when you phoned about an hour back. In fact, I answered first.'

Tina pushed a new cigarette into her holder. But she did not attempt to light it.

'You sure do get around.'

'Yeah . . . but that doesn't mean I move in circles. Why are you framing that kid Farrel with the slaying of Daks?'

Tina said softly: 'Get me a drink.'

She was playing along for time. Tearle poured her a rum neat. He didn't know whether she drank rum neat, but it seemed suitable. Then he repeated the question.

'You're plumb crazy,' she told him. 'I can't frame anyone. The cops do that sort of work.'

'Sure. And right now you're giving the cops plenty of assistance. Let's get this set-up right. Daks was murdered last night. At about the same time this kid called Farrel was seen leaving the house — leaving in a hurry. Tonight he was spending dough that they say was taken from Daks either before or after he was killed. So he's arrested. None of this adds

41

up. You don't have to be an Einstein to know that. This, sister, is the clearest frame-up I've hit. And your call to Cullen confirmed it.'

She swallowed the neat rum. The drink seemed quite suitable. Then she said: 'You're doing all the talking. Carry on. I'm getting interested. What do you figure's behind all this?'

Tearle didn't feel like it, but he gave her a grin. The sort of grin that would make any girl sore. Even a girl like Tina.

'That isn't so hard to answer — not since you told me you plan to take over Daks' mob. Maybe it was you who arranged the killing so you could put your dainty little feet right into your boyfriend's shoes. And it could be that you and Cullen are framing Farrel so as to put you in the clear. I always knew Cullen was a crooked cop, but I figure there must be a big cut in this for him, or it just wouldn't be worth his while.'

Tina stood up. She faced Tearle for a few seconds. Then she glided towards him, her white evening dress glistening under the strong lights.

'You're getting smart. Maybe you're getting too smart. And now what do you intend doing about it?'

'I work for a newspaper. I can still write a nice story.'

Tina laughed. A soft laugh and without humour.

'Maybe we can look after that side of it, too.'

They were so close to each other that you couldn't have squeezed a hand between them when Tearle said: 'What makes you think you can control an outfit like this, Tina?'

She ran the tip of her tongue along her lips. Like a cat thinking about a meal.

'Daks was a nice guy. He had a lot of dough. And he didn't keep it in a bank.'

Tearle understood. If Tina had that dough and only she knew where it was, she'd be able to run the mob okay.

'You're sitting nice and pretty,' he told her. 'And I guess you can go on that way . . . for a few days . . . until the mob find where you've tucked the wad.'

Her voice came in a hiss.

'I ain't that dumb. I don't keep that

43

kinda money in my stocking. Get this — I'm a girl, but I can run this kinda organisation just as well as any guy in pants. Maybe better. Before I'm through I plan to really make something outa this city and I plan to do it fast. You'll be surprised how fast. I've got plenty of co-operation arranged in the right places and nothing's gonna stop me. Not even a hick reporter.'

She didn't look so good right now. She was taut and there was a sort of evil about her. Eyes were staring and her teeth showed small and pointed between her stretched lips.

Tearle was thinking hard. Thinking of just what might happen in Vallis City if a crazed woman got loose with a lot of dough and a mob of killers. Maybe that was why he didn't notice her press a wall bell.

He only stopped concentrating on the future when the door opened and Hal came in. Hal was a hoodlum, and very tough. Peace loving citizens got out of the way when they saw Hal around. Hal could crush a normal man's ribs by pressing them with his hands. He had done just that, and more than once.

Right now, Hal was standing on the threshold and the crown of his fuzzed head was not so many inches short of the top of the door. He was watching Tina. Waiting for her to speak. Like some huge dog awaiting a word of command.

Tina said to him: 'Strap up this punk. I'm gonna work on him myself. I'm gonna convince him that from now on his best policy is to forget all about us.'

She had a pearl handled Derringer in her hand. Tearle was looking direct into its muzzle.

4

A Little Treatment

At the moment when Tearle was absorbing the details of the gun he was also subconsciously aware of a movement behind him. He guessed it was Ivan waking. It was a good guess. Ivan was pulling himself upright. He didn't look so good. He reeled a bit as he eased towards Tina.

Tina gave him a quick glance.

'Go take a rest,' she told him. 'Hal and me's gonna be busy in the next few minutes. We don't want any invalids around.'

Ivan's pan was the hue of a bad egg yolk.

'I wanta stay right here. I've a personal interest in this guy.'

Tina gave a slight shrug of her shoulders.

'Okay — if you figure you can take it.

But you haven't shown up so good up to now.'

There was a dull burning in the depth of Tearle's belly. That's where nerve reactions are always felt first. In the depth of the belly. And he was suffering from plenty of nerve reaction.

He was starting to wonder whether he'd been so smart in coming along to this place. He'd got a good story for the paper, anyway. But maybe it was not only a story that he was after. Maybe he was kind of interested in that kid Farrel. He didn't go for that kind of frame up. And it was only a mild sample of what could follow if Tina got to work in the city. Particularly now she had Cullen tied up nice and snug.

Tearle decided to start talking again. This was no time for heroics. Heroes don't live so long. And you're not so useful when you're dead.

'I'll forget about you,' he lied. 'There's no need to get physical about it. I guess I know when to call off. This is too big for me.'

Tina wasn't impressed any. One of her

47

arched eyebrows went up a fraction. It gave her a satanic kind of look.

'You're yellow. You're scared of what's coming.'

Tearle thought that that was no sin. Any guy would have been scared. But he said: 'I guess if I write this story I'll stop a slug . . . okay . . . I can understand that without any of the muscle technique.'

'Maybe. But the treatment I've got in mind for you will push the lesson home.'

Tearle remembered that somewhere at some time he'd read that a wise guy of a long time ago said a woman with power was more dangerous than a thousand serpents. That sage sure did know his stuff. Tina was clever, ambitious. You could see that she was savouring the prospect of what she was planning to do to him.

It was Ivan who offered him his chance. He took it.

Ivan was still swaying a bit. As if he was alone in a gale. And that wasn't any discredit. Not when you've been slugged with a table top. But right now he was within reach of Tearle. And he was looking in a detached sort of way at Hal.

Tearle balanced on his left foot and pushed out his right shoe hard. It contacted Ivan on the ankle. Ivan made a noise like a defective sink and he spun backwards towards Tina. Ivan was having a rough day. Maybe he should have read his horoscope in the *Tribune* and followed the advice to take things quietly for the next twenty-four hours.

His movement towards Tina put him between her and Tearle. And Tearle didn't wait. He slapped his right mitt into Ivan's mug. Deliberately, the blow landed high and in the region of the forehead. This forced Ivan further back so that he crashed into Tina.

But Tina did not take the full force of the impact. She'd half squirmed away. But it was enough to knock her partly off balance. It was in the second of confusion that Tearle made a long jump. It carried him past Ivan and to Tina's side. Her gun was waving, He gripped the wrist holding it.

It was a slender wrist, but it had plenty of strength. Even so, she could not resist the intolerable application of pain. Her fingers relaxed and Tearle dragged the Derringer from her.

But now Hal was moving up.

It had taken time for Hal to get a grip on this situation. Some hoods are quick witted and have good brains. Hal was not one of them. He liked to have breathing space to sort things out. Right now, he'd had his breathing space, and he was lumbering forward, groping under his jacket for the Luger that hung in a shoulder holster.

Tearle saw him coming. He jabbed the Derringer between Tina's shoulder blades. She was wearing a low cut evening dress and the muzzle made a white mark on her bare flesh.

'Stop just where you are,' he said. 'If you pull out that gun then this dame'll stop a slug.'

At first it looked as if Hal was going to ignore the threat. His mitt went on feeling under his jacket. Then the meaning of the words penetrated the bone and tissue. He paused, hand on the Luger butt, looking helplessly at Tina.

Tearle decided it was time to help Tina along.

'Tell these punks to get outa here,' he said, his mouth only an inch from her ear. 'I'm still wanting to have that talk with you. But with all this company I guess we're apt to be disturbed. It spoils the concentration.'

Tina did not argue. Folks who argue while they have a gun in their backs are all dead — or they are due to die soon.

She said: 'Okay boys. Get out. I'll deal with this slob myself.'

Her voice was level and controlled. Tearle decided that Tina had plenty of nerve. Maybe from her point of view that was a good thing. Nerve was what she was going to need.

There was another period of hesitation from Hal. Tearle, standing direct behind Tina, could not see her face. But she must have said something in dumb show, because Hal suddenly nodded. He went out of the room. Ivan followed.

There was a long settee near the fireplace. Tearle put a hand on to Tina's back and pushed her towards it. She fell

51

forward among the cushions. Then he crossed to the door. A key was in the lock and he turned it.

Tina stayed where he had pushed her, lying full length. But she was following Tearle's movements. Following them with a sort of icy interest.

Tearle kept the Derringer in his mitt. He guessed that was a desirable precaution. He didn't want to be involved in a wrestling bout with Tina.

Tearle gave himself another drink. He figured he deserved it. Tina still watched as the rye went down.

It was after quite an interval of silence that he said: 'How did you frame that kid Farrel?'

She didn't answer. And she didn't look as though she intended to answer.

Tearle tried again.

'How did you fix it so he climbed over the walls of this house at just about the time Daks was killed? And who is he, anyway?'

She was still silent.

Tearle glanced at the Derringer. It was comforting to have it ready in his hand.

Particularly since Ivan and Hal could be sending out a signal for some more of the mob. When they arrived there was likely to be real trouble.

But he decided to risk putting it away for a time. For the sort of work he had in mind, the gun would be in the way.

He dropped it into his side pocket. Then he stood direct over Tina. Now she'd twisted her head so she was looking up at him. There was an inferno in her dark eyes.

Tearle said: 'You were gonna work on me, but there's been a hitch. Life's full of hitches, sister. For instance, ten minutes ago you'd never have thought that I'd be handing out a little treatment to you. But that's just what I'm going to do until you give me all you know about Farrel . . . '

He grabbed a fist-full of her hair. It was strong, it was wiry, and it gave out a faint whiff of perfume; he pulled hard. Tina was dragged off the settee and on to her feet so that she was facing him.

Still holding a fist-full of her crowning glory, Tearle whipped the back of his hand across her cheek. She tried to move away, but she could not. The blow left a red mark. But she made no sound.

Tina did not break so easy. In fact, Tina had never been known to break. The mob boys still talked about the time she pulled a slug out of her own arm — a slug from a cop's gun. No doctor was around and she just didn't trust anyone else to do the work. Tina was that sort of dame.

And Tearle was starting to realise it. Beginning to wonder just what he'd have to do to make her sing. He didn't want to have to go too far. He was one hundred per cent in favour of old world courtesy so far as women were concerned. Even women like Tina. But maybe he'd have to forget those nice scruples . . .

He did not have to forget them. Tina changed. Her whole attitude changed. It was as though she'd moved some master switch that controlled her personality. A switch that had changed her from a spitting she-cat to a docile doll.

She whispered: 'Okay . . . we'll talk. Maybe it's the best thing to do. Sometimes rough play's useful. But not now. Not while I'm at the receiving end of it.'

There was something more than that sudden softness about her. There was a faint glimmer of humour, too, as she gave out the last sentence.

Tearle let go her hair. Her face came forward. There was perfume in her breath, too. A heavy, sultry sort of perfume. It came to him when she spoke again. It was still a whisper.

She said: 'We're playing this the wrong way. I told you before I like my guys rough. We two could make nice music. How about calling off the feudin'?'

Tearle thought: 'Hell . . . she's throwing me old bait . . .'

'I ain't falling for this delaying action, sister. Do you tell me what I want to know?'

He got the right ring into his voice. She leaned slightly away from him, but her arms were round his shoulders. And there was that faint smile on her rich lips. The smile that had everything except humour.

'What's your interest in that hick?'

'I've got plenty of interest and I ain't going to watch him lifted into any hot seat.'

She gave out a soft laugh.

'He won't. Why don't you get wise? That kid'll stick around in jail for a few weeks maybe, but he'll have to be released in the end. Then he'll be okay and he'll have acted as a nice cover for . . . for the guy who slew Daks.'

Tearle wrenched his arms away, and he didn't do it gently.

'You're making me sick. But get this . . . I'm gonna write up just everything I know about Daks and you and the rest of the lousy set-up. And no threats of bullets is gonna stop me. I have a hunch I'll be able to look after myself. Anyway, it wouldn't look so good for you if I stop a slug after writing that story. Folks might get kinda suspicious. Even Cullen might be forced to do something.'

There was an unusual wideness about her oval eyes and she wasn't smiling any more.

Tina said: 'You're not being so smart. That's because you don't know the pitch. Not all of it. But while you were lugging at my hair I came to a decision. I'm like that — I come to fast decisions in odd places. This time, I thought maybe it'd be a waste to see a guy like you come to any harm. A guy with your nerve. And brain, too. That's what I like most. You've got something besides marrowbone inside your skull. And mental power — that's a rare asset and I don't come across much of it. I could use it. I could use your newspaper experience, too. So think it over . . . '

She was talking briskly and seriously. She broke off to find her cigarette-holder. It was on the carpet She continued when she was smoking again.

'You can leave this house without being touched. If you have any doubts, you can walk out with a gun in my back. That way, you'll be safe. But don't play tough with me. Think over what I've said. If you're gonna play ball, give me a call at ten o'clock. I'll be waiting. And I don't usually wait for guys to call me . . . '

5

The arrest

It was around midday when Tearle awoke in his apartment. He had not broken his sleep to make any telephone calls. But right now someone was trying to call him.

Sun rays were cutting through the windows and the phone at his bedside was ringing. Hyman was at the other end of the wire. And Hyman didn't sound as though he was enjoying the warm summer day. His tones cut like a rusted razor.

'Where the hell did you get to last night?' he wanted to know. 'We kept half a column free for your story and what happens? I'll tell you. We get no story and the last edition starts rolling ten minutes late, all on account of you.'

Tearle told him to cool off.

'It wasn't all that easy. But I've got a story now and it's big stuff. I want to check one or two facts first then I'll be in the office to write it this afternoon.'

Hyman was a bit mollified.

'Okay. But it'd better be good. There are a whole lot of rumours going around since Daks died and folks are looking to us to give them the truth. Don't get lost this time. You're a big boy now and you ought to be learning to find your way around.'

Tearle put back the receiver and gave himself a cigarette.

Then he decided that maybe he'd like to eat. His apartment was in a big block and room service was provided. He phoned down for coffee, ham and eggs. After that he felt better. And he felt better still after a bath and shave.

On the way down in the elevator the bellhop said: 'I see the cops have got the guy who killed Daks. That sure was quick work to pull him in like that. But he must have been dumb to hang around town. I guess that story's cold until the trial comes up.'

Tearle told him he guessed it was, too. But the bellhop wanted to talk some more. He said: 'It ain't so safe to talk much about Daks' mob. But in my line of business you hear a whole lot of things. I gotta a pal who's porter at the Arcadian Hotel. Captain Cullen goes in there a lot. Maybe you'd like to know what my pal saw . . .'

'Maybe I would,' Tearle told him. 'You've got all of my attention.'

The bellhop was enjoying himself. He looked around as if to be sure no one else was listening. Then he said:

'Cullen's been meeting Dak's girl in there. That girl by the name of Tina.'

Tearle gave out a deep whistle. He said something, but the bellhop put him right.

'No. It wasn't that way. They just sat together in a corner of the foyer. They tried to act like they met by accident. But it wasn't any accident. We know in this line of business.'

'When did they meet?'

'Three — maybe four times. The last was about a week ago. It got the staff at the Arcadian talkin'.'

'And it looked like they were discussing something confidential?'

'It sure did, brother. They stopped talkin' every time anyone came near.'

Tearle gave the bellhop a buck. Then he eased out into the street.

He left his coupé in a public garage at the back of the apartment block. He started to move in that direction. But he didn't cover more than half a dozen paces. He stopped when a couple of men crowded in on either side of him. One of them was Lieutenant Bakana. Bakana looked at him with eyes that might have belonged to a dead musk rat. Tearle said: 'I'm not looking for company.'

Bakana had an unlighted cheroot inserted into his pan. He rolled it about his lips.

'But we are. We want your company, and that ain't on account of your charming personality. Cullen wants to see you bad.'

The other flatfoot had closed his hand over Tearle's arm. He did it in a serious kind of way.

'Yeah. Well I don't feel the same way about Cullen. Tell him I'll see him when I'm not so busy.'

Bakana said: 'You don't have to worry. You ain't gonna be busy. Cullen's planning to look after you for a long time.'

Tearle felt a surge of temper coming up. He wanted to do something about this slob. Something physical and drastic. It was hard work to resist the impulse.

His voice was frozen as he said: 'Cullen ain't cooking up anything on me. I ain't some innocent kid in a big city. Maybe I'd better come with you just so I can tell that creep exactly what I mean.'

'You're getting wise,' Bakana told him. 'Cullen ain't so sensitive. He'll survive listening to you.'

A patrol car was parked against the sidewalk. They got into it. Tearle sat in the back between the two cops. Another couple of flatfoots were in the front.

Cullen was sitting on the edge of his desk. He was trying to clear out a stoppage in his pipe. He did not look up as Tearle entered. Just went on operating with his pocketknife. Tearle jerked his arm free from the escort and walked towards Cullen.

He said quickly but quietly: 'There's still a constitution in this country and it doesn't allow hick cops to pull in private citizens just because bums like you want to talk to them. You'd better have a good reason for this.'

Cullen kept up the concentration on his pipe. But his pan stretched into a slight grin.

'I've got a good reason. You're under arrest and the charge is aggravated assault and damage to property.'

He was still scraping at the pipe bowl.

Tearle gave himself time to absorb the information. It took quite a bit of time.

'How did you dream this charge up?'

'It ain't no dream. The evidence has been given by Miss Tina Tallan. It seems you went to her home and slugged her around. You slugged Ivan Rascwitz, too. And you damaged furniture . . . '

Now Cullen had forgotten about that pipe. He was looking direct at Tearle. And he had the look of a man who was enjoying himself.

Tearle told him to go on. He wanted to know more.

'There ain't any more.' Cullen said. 'Except that it's serious to knock a dame around.'

'Yeah,' Tearle breathed. 'I guess Suzette would agree with that. But you ain't all that smart. I'm not being held on this sort of phony rap. I want that telephone and I want to speak to my city editor.'

Cullen waved a hand at the instrument.

'Go right ahead. You won't get much aid outa him.'

When Tearle got through he heard Hyman clear his throat at the other end.

Then Hyman said: 'What the hell have you been doing? I've just had a call from Cullen. Are you crazy? He says you've been roughing up that dame who belonged to Daks. He doesn't like to do it, he says, but he's just got to hold you on a charge. Did you knock this broad around?'

'Yeah, but that ain't the whole story,' Tearle told him. 'Listen, I want . . . '

Hyman broke in.

'It's enough of the story. I don't want to know more. When this comes out in court it'll make the paper look like a hoodlums' holiday guide. I've always supported my reporters when they've worked their way into a jam. But I've not had anything like this before and it's a whole lot too much. You're fired. You have the air.'

There was something final about the click as he slapped back the receiver.

Cullen's grin was wider. But at first Tearle hardly saw him. He was thinking about Hyman. And he figured he couldn't blame him. He wasn't such a bad guy. There are no good city editors. But a lot of them were worse than Hyman. And Hyman didn't know the background. He wasn't a mind reader.

Cullen asked: 'Satisfied? Maybe you'll appreciate that you're in a tough spot. It don't pay to interfere too much.'

Tearle lighted a cigarette. He breathed out some of the smoke towards Cullen's pan.

He said: 'You're reaching too high, Cullen. A whole lot too high. That dame's plumb crazy and there's gonna be no pay-off for a cop who works in with her.'

Cullen had big fists. When they were

bunched they looked like they were ends of meat. They were bunched right now. And one of them travelled from his waist level towards Tearle's belly. It wasn't the sort of punch that'd get a man anywhere in a prize ring. Not even in a dirty prize ring.

It landed just two inches above the groin. It's there that you can do most damage.

At the moment of impact Tearle felt no pain. The nerves were paralysed. But hot and bitter liquid leapt up into the back of his throat and his eyes seemed to go out of focus.

Then the nerves recovered their feeling. Tearle groaned a bit and went slowly down to his knees. Cullen's voice seemed to come to him from some other dimension. It was loud then it was faint. It was deep then it was falsetto.

It said: 'This ain't any sorta place to relax, bud. Only kids play on the floor. You make this place look untidy. Get up.'

The toe end of his shoe planted itself into Tearles's ribs. A gong struck somewhere in the deep recesses of his head.

He listened to it reverberating as he passed out.

* * *

There's no comfort in a cop pound. Those boys don't believe in pampering prisoners. They believe that austerity is good for the conscience. Tearle found nothing in his surroundings to console him when he opened his eyes and immediately pressed a hand against his head. A head that seemed to be a concentration point for all the pain on Earth.

He was lying on a concrete floor. A bare wood bunk was hinged to one of the walls, but they hadn't bothered about laying him on that. That was a luxury.

The place consisted of three windowless walls and at the fourth end tall bars looked on to what seemed to be a corridor. Except for the bunk, there was no furniture.

After noting the details, he shut his eyes again, staying right where he was. He needed time for the head pain to lessen.

He was still lying there when the grill door was unlocked and someone came in. It was a uniformed cop. Tearle dragged himself upright. His head was not so bad now.

The cop pushed his cap back from his sweating forehead. He said: 'I sure am glad you're feeling okay. You've got yourself a visitor and when they come we like the residents to look good.'

Tearle fumbled in his pockets. Nothing there had been touched. Except the Derringer. Those cops had removed the artillery. But right now he wasn't so worried about the personal armament. He wanted a cigarette. The pack was crumpled. He drew a bent cigarette out.

His lighter was in his coat, but he said to the flatfoot: 'Give me a light.'

The cop gave him, one from a match which he struck on the wall.

'Who've I got as a visitor?'

The cop gave him a grin.

'You'll soon know. We like to surprise folks around this place.'

'Yeah,' Tearle said. 'I've noticed that.'

With the cop close behind him, he went

out into the corridor. Cells ran along both sides. Most were occupied. In one near the end he saw a fair-headed, pimpled kid asleep on his bunk.

Tearle asked: 'Would that be Farrel?'

The flatfoot did not reply. That was enough. Silence can provide a complete answer.

He was pushed through a door and into a room. It was a nicely furnished room — anyway, it seemed nice after that cell. There was a carpet and a couple of deep chairs. Not like a normal jail visiting room.

Tina was in one of those chairs. And she was alone.

Tearle thought: 'Jeeze . . . there's no denying she's got what it takes and some to spare.'

That was just the way Tina looked just then. She was in a tight turquoise costume. There was no sign of a bruise on her cheek. Maybe it was well covered with cosmetic. Or maybe Tearle hadn't hit her all that hard. She was looking straight at Tearle and that half-smile was on her lips.

The cop eased out.

Tina said: 'You look like you've had a tough time.'

Tearle did not answer. He was looking through the window. There were no bars on that window and it showed out on to a main street. Tina followed his eyes.

'You wouldn't get so far,' she told him evenly. 'But there's no need for you to think about that sort of thing. I figure it's no use asking you again if you'll play ball along with me. It's a solid, genuine offer . . . '

Tearle cut in: 'I don't play ball with the reptile species. It's dangerous.'

That didn't seem to affect her any.

'Then you sure are passing up a big chance of making a whole lot of dough. Me and the boys are gonna clean up big. But for me it gonna be just the beginning . . . '

Tearle chanced to glance at her eyes. He was chilled. Chilled by their hardness. Tina was dreaming into the future.

'I aim to hit a new town soon. In a new country. And I intend to hit it in a big way. The sorta dough I'll have will make that easy.'

She spoke as though the prospect were very close. Tearle asked: 'Just which country and which town's gonna have the pleasure of your company?'

'I dunno — yet. I'm not in any hurry. But when I find the right place I'm gonna take it over as a running concern. And it's gonna keep on running — my way. Even the local newspaper . . . That's one special reason why I'd like to work in with you. Newspapers can be a nuisance. They can also be an asset. I plan to buy up the local sheet. You could run it for me. I've heard that journalists don't always play the way their publisher would like. But you could make sure that doesn't happen to me. You could if you were editor. Control of a newspaper would give me control of a town.'

Tearle thought: 'She's crazy all right.' But he said:

'You sound like you've got something real big planned, Tina.'

It was a hook, but she didn't bite.

'Maybe. You could find out all about that if you throw in with me. But not unless.'

71

'Is that your only reason for coming here . . . to throw me another invitation? I figured you got me arrested because I didn't phone you this morning. Well, I still ain't dangling on your string, so what's your next move, sister?'

She pulled at her cigarette. Then she said: 'I'm also here to tell you that you can quit this jail.'

Tearle swivelled round. The gong started in his head again. Not so loud as when Cullen had kicked him, but loud enough.

'Are you kidding? You have me arrested so I can't write the story, then you tell me I can go . . . what's the pay-off?'

'No pay-off. I figure it's good diplomacy. By now you've seen enough to know you can't play tough with me. But I still want your cooperation. I still aim to get it. But I won't get it so easy while you're cookin' in a cell. So I'm gonna let you leave here — only there are a couple of conditions.'

Tearle played his piece. He asked her about the conditions.

She said: 'You've gotta undertake to

keep your kisser buttoned up. And you've gotta resign yourself to the idea that some of my mob'll be right on your tail — just to see you behave.'

Tearle's cigarette didn't taste so good. A bit like rotted hay.

'And if I don't do that?'

'Then you'll stay right here as a guest of Captain Cullen. But not for long. We don't want you coming up in court and shooting your mouth off. Before that happens you'll have an accident. A serious accident. And you won't recover. Cullen'll fix that. Get me?'

Tearle told her that he got it.

He said: 'I ain't the only newspaper-man around here. Others can get on to what's happening. Sooner or later the story'll break and the Federal men will move in on a clean up.'

She was smiling now. Lips parted and curved up. That glitter of amusement in her eyes.

'Sure . . . that's bound to happen. But not yet, And the operation I'm planning ain't gonna be delayed for so long . . . '

She put a hand on his elbow.

'Right now, nothing can touch me. Even if you put over the story to the *Tribune* it wouldn't change the pitch. They've fired you, haven't they? Do you think they'd believe you? They wouldn't, Mister Tearle. They'd figure you'd gone plumb crazy. But all the same, it'd be healthier for you if you keep nice and quiet and think about my proposition. Just stick around town for the next few hours. Visit the museum. Go look at the art gallery. Take it quietly. I'll be contacting you, and next time I hope you won't pass up the prospect of working in with me. I ain't kidding when I say I aim to buy a newspaper. You'd look good and pretty in an editor's chair . . .'

She moved towards the door. Long, unhurried strides, like she was floating. Before she went out she turned and said: 'And don't forget. From the time you leave this building my boys'll be watching you. If you're thinking of a double-cross, you just ain't got a chance.'

6

The Slob with a Knife

Nothing moves faster than thought. That's why it took Tearle no more than five minutes to figure out all the prospects and reach a decision. Those five minutes were spent in walking from headquarters back to his apartment.

The bellhop was surprised.

'You ain't been out so long, Mr. Tearle. Maybe you forgot something, eh?'

Tearle glanced across the lobby to the street entrance. It was as he'd expected. Ivan was there. Ivan and a couple of other slobs who were too far back to be identified. They were doing the tailing.

'Yeah, I forgot something,' Tearle told him. As they eased into the elevator, Ivan sat himself in the lobby. Ivan wasn't taking chances.

In his apartment, Tearle picked up the phone. He was making an experiment. He asked the block operator for the *Tribune* number. The operator said: 'I'm sorry. I can't put that one through. I can't put any of your calls through. It's police headquarters orders. No calls of yours have to be handled.'

The woman sounded genuinely apologetic. Puzzled, too. And maybe a bit scared.

'Don't worry,' Tearle told her. 'The cops just don't want me to strain myself.'

He gave himself a drink. He figured that Tina and Cullen had rigged the pitch nicely.

There were other folks in the block who would be glad to let him use their telephones. But all calls had to go through the block operator. As soon as she recognised his voice she'd cut him off. Maybe he could get someone else to speak for him, but that would sound even more crazy to the boys in the *Tribune* office. Anyway, it was almost certain that all calls to the newspaper would be banned, whoever made them.

And he couldn't use a phone outside the apartment. He'd have Ivan's close company just as soon as he attempted that. But he wanted to get hold of a man at the office. A man named Dugan. Another reporter. Maybe the only one who could help him.

It was all working out the way he'd figured. The project he'd thought up on his walk from headquarters would have to be put into operation.

Tearle eased into his bedroom and unlocked a drawer. There was a gun there, a war relic. He took it out, inserted a clip of six shells into the magazine and dropped it in his jacket pocket. That made him feel a whole lot better. After giving himself another long drink he eased out of the apartment. Ivan was in the corridor. And Ivan was looking mean. Tearle gave him a grin.

He said: 'I'm gonna help you, Ivan. I'm gonna let you know just what I'm aiming to do. Right now, I'm on the way down to the lobby and there I'm gonna have a coffee. After that I may take a drive in my car just to clear my head.'

Ivan didn't look grateful. He moved his big shoulders.

'Don't try going too far or too fast. That's just a friendly kinda warning, because it wouldn't worry me none to put a slug into you.'

Tearle was still grinning when he said: 'Buddy, that's one feeling we both have in common . . .'

They went down together in the elevator. The bellhop was looking still more surprised. He'd just heard about the ban on the phone calls. But he didn't talk. There was something about Ivan that didn't encourage conversation.

Tearle ordered his coffee and Ivan sat at a nearby table watching. It was like trying to relax in the company of a Congo ape. But Tearle did not hurry. He wanted to give the impression that he was taking it all the easy way. He even looked through some magazines before getting up and moving into the street.

This time he got to the garage where his coupé was parked. But he didn't back it out right away. Instead he spent several minutes just letting the engine run so it would be good and warm when it hit the road.

As he eased into the main street a big saloon tucked in right behind him. The mob were still keeping company.

But not for long.

There was a heavy transport truck right ahead. Tearle pulled out then squeezed in front of it, placing the vehicle between him and the saloon. Then he switched down a side road.

The sun was going down and he had temporarily lost the mob car when he hit the desert road out of Vallis City. Then he pressed his foot on the gas pedal and kept it there. There was no prospect of shaking the saloon off for good. A check with the cops would soon put those boys on to the route he had taken, even if they hadn't eventually seen him themselves. But he'd got himself a start. And a start was all he wanted. It was one hell of a drive, and the moon was high when he braked outside of a long, white building that was surrounded by artificial lawns. This was Frisco's Desert Club.

Before getting out of the car, Tearle glanced at the trip indicator. It showed that he'd covered just on a hundred miles and he'd taken just on ninety minutes to do it. He figured that he now had at least ten minutes in hand before the saloon came up. He thought of concealing his own coupé, but dismissed the notion. This was the first stopping place on the road out of Vallis and Ivan would be sure to make a check here.

Right now, sand was in his hair, in his clothes, in his throat. Most of all it was in his throat. He intended doing something about that — after he'd used the phone.

Inside, a few folks were flopping around a small dance square to the music of a band. But most of the customers were at the bar. The night was a whole lot too warm for much physical exercise.

Frisco's was not a spot that people went to for entertainment. It was mostly used by travellers who wanted a bed for the night. But there was a small town five miles off and the fashionable citizens there sometimes came out to Frisco's to eat and drink. Mostly to drink. A few of them were there when Tearle eased in.

He had visited the place before — mostly when covering assignments.

But it had been quite a time since his last visit. When Frisco saw him he left the bar and gripped Tearle's band.

Frisco was a Sicilian. He was a little man with a big moustache which stood out at each end of his pan as if he'd had an electric shock. For the last ten years he'd been working towards getting a certificate of United States citizenship, But so far he hadn't succeeded. Not that there was much wrong with Frisco. In fact, he was a good sort of guy. But to become an American citizen it's necessary to pass a written test in English. Frisco hadn't been able to manage that test. It could be that he left Sicily too late in life to learn another language.

'I see you good,' he told Tearle. 'Have I to put up weeth you?'

Tearle told him that he sure did want to be put up. For one night, or maybe two.

Tearle moved in on the bar. He ordered a tall rye and drank it fast. Then he went to the phone box which was in a corner. He gave the operator the number of the *Tribune*.

There was a couple of minutes' wait

until the *Tribune* came through. He told the operator to put him through to the news room. He said he wanted to speak to Hugh Dugan.

There was another wait and this one was anxious. Time was slipping. Maybe he shouldn't have had that drink, but it had seemed a vital refreshment at the time. Dugan was just the sort of guy he wanted to contact. Dugan was not only a good reporter. He didn't scare easy, either. And when he wasn't embracing a bottle of rye, he had a quick and clear brain. It'd be too bad if he wasn't around.

But he was around. He sounded excited when he heard Tearle's voice.

'Say, I've been trying to contact you at police headquarters, but that slob Cullen had you fenced off. I didn't know you'd been sprung. Where are you now?'

'I haven't been sprung,' Tearle told him. 'I've been officially released. The charge against me's been dropped.'

He told Dugan where he was. Dugan knew the Desert Club okay. Then Tearle said: 'I want you to come out here, without saying anything about it to anyone. It's urgent, or I wouldn't ask. I need help and I need it bad.'

Dugan said: 'Sure I'll come out. But what the hell are you doing out there?'

Tearle told him he'd know when he arrived. He was taking in a breath to add another sentence. But he paused. There was a mirror in the booth. In it he saw a reflection. A reflection of three punks gathered close round the door.

Ivan and his assistants had arrived. They were not attempting to enter the booth. They were just leaning up and listening to him through the thin glass panels. Something in Tearle's head whispered: 'This is it. You gotta keep calm. You gotta go on acting like you haven't seen them. You gotta make them think you're unarmed.'

Then he went on speaking to Dugan. And he raised his voice a bit, so it could be clearly heard.

He said: 'There's one thing more I want you to do. Can you bring a gun with you? I need a gun bad. Right now I've got nothing to defend myself with but my personality.'

There was a long pause.

'A gun . . . Jeeze, what are you doing? Ain't one assault charge enough? What do you want with a gun?'

'I don't want it for an ornament. But this is urgent — can you bring one?'

He could picture Dugan's red and perplexed pan. Dugan answered doubtfully: 'I don't know that I can help. I don't keep artillery because I've never needed any. But maybe I can borrow one . . . I don't know, though . . . '

Tearle cut in: 'That's fine. Bring it along. Scrape the rust off and load it with shells. I'll feel a whole lot more wholesome when that Luger's in my hands.'

Dugan breathed heavily at the other end. He said: 'What the hell are you bleatin' about. I ain't got any Luger. I just told you I ain't got a gun.'

But Tearle hooked the receiver.

He stayed in the booth for another full minute. He used the time in flipping through the numbers directory. like he was going to make another call. But that was a blind. He wanted to regroup his wits. To steady his morale. Right now. his morale wasn't in such good shape.

That booth had become a trap. A trap from which there might be no escape. His hand was in his jacket pocket, gripping the Colt when he pushed open the door and eased out.

There were only three of them, but it was like walking into a crowd at a ball game. They made a tight circle round Tearle. A solid ring of muscle. Tearle fixed on Ivan.

'You sure seem to like my company,' he told him. 'I told you I was gonna take a ride. What's your worry?'

Ivan's flat and expressionless eyes bored through him. Tearle took a quick gander at the others. He recognised both. The one who was placing a foot over his own so he couldn't easily move, was Aarga. A knifeman. Not that he threw them. Aarga was smart with the four-inch blade he kept strapped up his left wrist. The other was Pretty. That was what they called him. And he was pretty, too, if you go for punks with bleached waves in their hair and the heart of a rat.

Ivan said: 'It wasn't so smart of you to send out for help. We figured you might start doing just that. It sure was tough on you that we saw you easing into the booth as we were comin' in.'

Aarga was increasing the pressure on his foot. He was placing most of his weight on the soft leather behind the shoe cap. And there was a tight sort of grin on Aarga's pan as he was doing it. It didn't improve his looks any. Aarga had one of those thin and high-boned mugs that make a normal man wonder what the hell his parents had looked like.

Tearle decided this was not the time to play soft. That policy wouldn't pay off. He took a hold of a fistful of Aarga's coat lapels. It was a line in mustard coloured coats and it was new.

'Try standing on the floor,' Tearle told him. 'You'll find it a whole lot safer.'

He twisted his wrist and Aarga, a bit off balance, stepped back. But there was hell, pure hell, in his eyes.

But Ivan wasn't taking much notice of Aarga. He was still watching Tearle.

He said: 'You're coming along with us.

We're gonna find a nice quiet place and we're gonna fix you good. Tina shouldn't have let you outa that cell. That girl was crazy to think she could use you. But I guess she'll be glad when she knows about this. We're gonna save us all a whole lot of trouble.'

'You're kinda optimistic,' Tearle told him. 'Tina didn't give any order for me to be fixed. My guess is she won't like punks who work on their own.'

Ivan hitched those big shoulders. That movement expressed a lot.

He said: 'Yeah, and so what? She's got the key to the big dough, so we string along with her. And she's got influence. The sorta influence that's gonna mean a whole lot . . . soon, too. After that — maybe we'll be through with her.'

Tearle thought: 'That's how I figured it. That's what I told the dame.'

And it was. That mob'd rather work with a Kentucky potman than any girl. Even a girl like Tina. She might fix a smooth deal with Cullen, whatever it was, but that wouldn't help her any when her own boys got to work on her.

Aarga said: 'What are we waiting for? Let's get this guy outa here. I don't want to spend the whole night in the desert.'

Ivan nodded.

He said: 'We know you ain't got a gun because we heard yer yellin' for one. But even if you had, you wouldn't stand a chance. You come quiet with us and we may make it easy for you. You'll get it quick — in the head. But start yelpin' and Aarga'll do the work. He'll do it with the blade.'

Tearle felt something touch his side. Something ice cold. He knew what it was. It was the edge of Aarga's knife. He'd pressed it through the clothing and the first half inch was in contact with the flesh.

But to look at Aarga, no one would know what he was doing. His left arm seemed to be hanging casually at his side, and just slightly pressing against Tearle. The steel wasn't visible, Aarga sure could handle a knife.

Ivan and Pretty were slightly in front as they moved across the bar and in the direction of the door. The folks were still dancing. The band was still raising melodious hell. The bar was still busy. But no one took any notice of them.

No one except Frisco. Frisco had been leaning against the bar talking to a customer. He looked surprised when he saw Tearle leaving. Still holding his drink, he hurried across to them. His round, dark face looked anxious.

'So early to leave,' he announced, putting himself direct in the path of Tearle and Aarga, so they had to stop. 'Ees it that you don't want this place? I hope you are not satisfied.'

He glanced curiously at Aarga. That was natural. Frisco's place was no class joint. But it was still not the sort of club where you'd expect to see Aarga's breed.

Tearle hesitated. Then he said: 'I'm okay. Just changed my mind about staying here. I have to leave in a hurry.' Ivan had come up. He put a hand on Frisco's fat shoulder. 'Don't worry. He's going a long way fast.'

The flesh round Frisco's mouth became taut. Maybe he didn't understand it all, but he knew something was wrong. Frisco was no linguist, but that didn't make him dumb.

He made a vague, helpless sort of gesture. But he showed no sign of moving. He was still blocking their path. Ivan was getting impatient. And Tearle felt a slight increase in the pressure of the blade.

'You heard . . . our friend's in a hurry. He won't be staying.'

Still the little guy didn't move. He wasn't yellow.

But Ivan had had enough. Frisco was holding his drink in his left hand. Ivan whipped up the edge of his fist. It caught the base of the tall glass and the liquid slapped into Frisco's eyes.

'Start movin',' Ivan said.

They were out of the club while Frisco was still trying to see.

The black saloon was near the main door. Tearle was eased into the back seat and sat there between Ivan and Aarga. Pretty took the wheel.

The dull throb of the engine drowned the faint sound of the dance music and the lights of the club faded as they hit the desert road.

They were moving back in the direction of Vallis City. Those boys felt they might as well do this work while on their way home.

The road was good and wide and the only traffic was an occasional long-distance haulage truck. They covered eight miles in the same number of minutes. Then Pretty started to ease off on the gas pedal. He kept looking out of the side windows. There was no scenery here. Only desert. Just sand and patches of cactus scrub.

Ivan said: 'Okay. This'll do.'

The Packard pulled into the side of the highway and braked. Ivan got out. Tearle followed with Aarga right behind him.

'We're taking a little walk first,' Ivan said. 'Just to get a nice distance away from the road. It don't look so good for respectable travellers to see a dead guy on the sand. It might upset them. Some people are sorta sensitive.'

Aargo pushed with the knife. This time it was enough to pierce the skin. But he didn't worry about it. His brain was on ice. He figured that if he was going to have any chance of reaching old age it would have to stay that way.

The Colt was still in his pocket. And his right hand was still over the butt. Just as it had been when he left the phone booth. It hadn't moved.

It was certain that when the moment came they would let him walk a few paces ahead before giving it to him. That would be his chance. His only chance,

The surprise effect would help. He might be able to drop to the sand and shoot first . . . might . . .

Then Ivan's voice came to him again. It said: 'We've changed our plans. We figure maybe a slug'd be too noisy. Someone might hear an' get scared. Aarga'll fix you. He'll do it with his blade. Ain't that so, Aarga?'

7

Bequest from Aarga

It shouldn't have been any sort of surprise. It was natural. Even if there'd been no chance of a shot being heard from the highway, those creeps would still have plumbed for the knife method.

Tearle told himself that he was forgetting what kind of hoodlums these were. He'd been expecting too much from them. He'd been expecting that they'd try to hand him it quickly. But they were planning it slow.

Their shoes made a faint crunch on the rock and sand. That was all. That was the only sound. High up, the moon was travelling fast and making patches of light and shade. Like it was setting the scene for an open-air morgue.

The sweat pores in Tearle's hands were wide open and they were releasing a deep flow of hot grease. Particularly in his right hand. The hand that held the Colt.

That Colt could still be used.

The knife was pressed low against his stomach. For that sort of work Aarga always used his left hand. And the gun was in his jacket pocket — directly over the knife. There was maybe a couple of inches separating them.

Ivan said: 'This is okay. You can give it to him now.'

Aarga's arm tensed. He didn't get any further than that.

Tearle fired through his pocket.

The slug tore through the lining and hit the ground near his feet. It had lost most of its force by then. On the way it it had met a tough obstacle. That obstacle had been Aarga's knuckles.

He gave out a long and trembling kind of squeal. It blended with the echo of the cartridge. And then Aarga held up a blooded mess of flesh and splintered bone that had been his hand. It wouldn't be a hand again.

But he didn't have much time to inspect it. Inside another second Tearle was round the back of him and holding him round the waist so he acted as a shield. A living, quivering shield. And he levelled the Colt at Ivan.

Ivan was no distance off. No more than ten yards. Pretty was standing just a bit further away.

It was easy shooting range, in good visibility. But this visibility was not so good. The light and shade made accurate aim difficult.

And that was fortunate for Tearle.

Fortunate because Ivan sent over the first slug.

He must have had his artillery ready in his hand when they left the car. In the ordinary way, Ivan didn't think so fast. His gun gave out a brief flash. There was a breath of displaced air near Tearle's head as the cylinder of lead whined past his shoulder.

Tearle threw Aarga flat on the sand and went down with him. Then he squeezed the trigger of the Colt. The gun gave a slight kick and the noise of its report seemed feeble after the row made by Ivan's heavier rod.

There was another flash. Not from

Ivan, this time. It came from Pretty. But Pretty's shot was yards wide.

Ivan bawled at Pretty: 'Get down and keep shooting till we've picked him off.'

They dropped to the sand and became almost invisible. Just dark hulks.

But Ivan provided the bigger hulk. Tearle figured he might be able to get him — if he took time. But he wasn't granted the time.

Aarga started to struggle.

Tearle had been lying behind Aarga, with an arm over his neck. At first the rat hadn't moved. Just groaned. He'd been too scared to do anything else. But now he'd got some of his nerve back. Maybe it was the realization that he was direct in the line of fire that helped him. He twisted and rolled from Tearle's loose grip, then with his good right hand he grabbed for the Colt.

And he got hold of the barrel.

There was a whole lot of strength in that hand. He held on to the gun like a vice. And his voice screamed through the night: 'Come and get him . . . I'm holdin' his rod . . . '

Tearle pulled at the butt with all he'd got. But Aarga moved with it.

There was only one answer to this. It had to be done. Tearle jerked the gun so that for a moment it was pointing at Aarga's chest. Then he pulled the trigger.

There was a click, The Colt had misfired.

Tearle breathed out a short oath. Most likely the shell was not seated square in the breech. It could have been caused by the pulling that was going on. If that was so, it'd take a full minute to clear the stoppage. And a minute was at least fifty seconds too long. For Ivan and Pretty were already getting to their feet before rushing towards him.

The only prospect now lay in running. Running deep into the desert and hoping that those punks were not so fast on their feet. But first he had to get rid of Aarga.

He bunched his left hand and gave it to the knifeman under the point of the jawbone. From that position — almost flat on the ground — it could not be a very hard punch. But it was enough for Aarga. The knifeman had been showing a kind of hysterical strength. But all the time he'd been losing blood. Now he had no reserves. The blow sent him out good and cold.

Tearle let go the Colt and coiled himself for the run.

But now there was a new sound.

It was a sound from the highway. A screech of brakes. And a blink of distant headlights. Far away, some guy was yelling. Then Ivan started to yell, too.

He bawled to Pretty: 'Back to the saloon . . .'

There was a sudden tightness around Tearle's throat. He knew just what had happened. Only one thing could have happened. One of those long-distance haulage trucks had been passing and heard the shooting. The crew were stopping for a check up. And some of those truck men were armed in case of hijackers. Ivan wasn't hanging around any longer. Right now, he and Pretty were running back towards the highway.

Deliberately, Tearle released the Colt from Aarga's fingers. He stood upright and concentrated on getting the gun back to shape. It had been like he thought. A badly seated cartridge. When the gun was ready again he put it in the coat pocket that had not been torn.

Then he looked carefully at Aarga.

And Aarga was on his way out.

His eyes were open now and he was conscious. But it was the sort of consciousness that doesn't last so long. The wound in his hand must have severed an artery.

He was looking up at the velvet sky in a glazed sort of way.

It was no more than a whispered croak when he said: 'They left me . . . Ivan and Pretty left me out here . . . the . . . '

There were dark blotches under his mouth. He was going fast. But he called on a last remnant of strength. And in those last moments he was hate — all hate for the men who'd left him.

'They're doin' the Western Allied Bank tomorrow . . . midday . . . Tina and Cullen fixed it . . . gonna be a million-dollar haul, then they're gonna clear out . . . Cullen, too. That's why we couldn't risk you quitting the city. But you can go to work now, big boy . . . I want you to fix those — '

He gave out a cough. A short and faint cough. Then he started to go cold. And his dead eyes were still watching the sky.

Tearle left him like that. And he eased towards the road.

The truck was there. Two haulage men were standing near it, looking along the highway. One of them pulled out a Colt as Tearle came up.

He asked: 'You in on the target practice, bud?'

'Yeah. I was the target.'

They looked at him like they weren't sure.

The man holding the gun said: 'Two bums just packed into a Packard and beat it towards Vallis City. They did it so fast we didn't have any chance of stopping them without shooting, and my work's to look after this truck. I ain't a cop.'

Tearle told him: 'They were trying to get tough with me. I ain't hurt, but that's only because you boys happened along.'

The driver asked: 'Hadn't we better take you to the cops?'

'Take me to Frisco's Club. That looks like it's on your route. I'll be able to get hold of any help I want from there.'

The truck men took him to the club. And on the way Tearle did some fast figuring about what Aarga had told him. About a snatch on the bank. And about Cullen helping to work it. Things sure looked like they were due to move in Vallis City.

8

The Big Deal

Frisco said: 'I thought I'd call out for the law. Then I thought not. I was high with worry.'

He still looked worried as he gave Tearle a drink from behind the now deserted bar.

'You did the right thing,' Tearle told him. 'I don't want to see any cops. Those guys didn't mean any harm. It was just by way of being a sorta misunderstanding.'

Frisco was doubtful. But he didn't ask any questions. Tearle didn't look like a man who'd welcome questions right now. He took himself to bed and left Tearle in the bar with a bottle of rye for company.

Tearle's strap watch showed that there was still an hour to go before Dugan was due to arrive. The bottle might last that time.

He was half-way down it when his eyes

started to close. It wasn't the liquor that was hitting him. It was just concentrated exhaustion. He fell asleep on the bar stool, head sprawled on the counter.

★ ★ ★

Dugan said: 'I didn't come out a hundred miles for the joy of watching you sleep off an overdose of rye.'

Then he slapped Tearle over the back.

Tearle heard the words and felt the slap at the same time. He opened heavy eyes and blinked. Dugan was grinning at him. Dugan didn't look like he'd been steam processed. He looked fresh after the drive through the night. His round and pink face was glistening. The sight of him made Tearle feel better. He wasn't alone any more.

Tearle said: 'I've fixed a room for you. But before we hit the hay we're gonna talk. Have a drink.'

He went behind the bar, found another glass. When they were both sitting on the tall stools Tearle gave it all. He didn't miss a thing. And while he was talking Dugan forgot to drink. Which meant he must have been mighty interested.

When he'd done Dugan whistled. Tearle allowed time for the basic facts to sink deep in. Then he said:

'Dying men don't lie. There's no sorta future in it. So I'm betting on what Aarga told me. And that means that this ain't gonna be any ordinary bank snatch. It's gonna be perfectly organised. Not a cop anywhere near the place when it happens. Cullen'll see to that. The bank and its staff are going to have as much chance as a colony of spring rabbits.

'Aarga talked about a million-dollar snatch. That could be right. The mob could clear enough to keep themselves on velvet for twenty years. Cullen included. You know, I thought Cullen was crazy to think a police chief could string along with a mob for long. But he's been smart. He doesn't intend to do it for long. He's working with them for just long enough to get some real dough. And that is until tomorrow midday.'

Dugan was looking a bit puzzled.

'How the hell did this dame manage to

keep control of the mob? And why did she have Daks killed?'

Tearle yawned.

'I have my ideas, but I'm keeping those to myself for a while. That's because I'm cautious and I could be wrong. But I'll tell you this. I know now that her story about sitting on Daks' dough is right enough. I figure the surprise will come when we find where it's kept.'

Dugan reminded him of Farrel. Tearle yawned again.

'The pitch has changed a lot in the last few hours. I've gotta go back to Vallis City — but not to get Farrel. That kid'll have to keep. There's no time to worry about him. I'm going to see Tina again.'

Dugan said: 'Jeeze . . . you sure are sticking that neck of yours out. You're not gonna last ten minutes after she sees you. Not after what she said.' Tearle gave himself a cigarette. 'I'm not figuring it that way. I think maybe she'll welcome me. She wanted me in her mob. She's gonna have me. I'm offering myself as a recruit. I'll pedal her a nice line about changing my mind. She doesn't know that Aarga told me about the bank raid, so it ought to go over smooth. It'll sorta flatter her. Then I'll see what can be done while you're talking fast and hard to the State governor.'

Dugan looked surprised. 'The State governor! Say, why should I go to see him? I don't know the guy so he ain't likely to listen if I talk.'

Tearle said: 'Get wise. You're independent. You haven't had any charge filed against you. So you're the very sorta guy he will listen to. You've gotta make him listen. If you don't, you'll be writing my obituary notice in the *Tribune* this time tomorrow. Now this is the way I'm gonna play Tina . . . '

He talked some more, but not a lot. When he'd done they left some folding money on the bar counter for Frisco.

It was three o'clock when they parted. Dugan taking the east route towards the Governor's residence, Tearle going back to Vallis City.

Tearle didn't hurry the trip. He wanted to get to Tina's place at around the time the servants would be getting up. Around six. He made it that way.

This time, he took his coupé right up the drive and parked it outside the main door. Then he went round to the back. There was some activity there. Not much, but some. A man in black pants and shirtsleeves was easing slowly about the kitchen. He was still half asleep and he didn't seem exactly delighted when Tearle came in. Tearle figured that this was one of the manservants.

'I've come to see Miss Tallan,' he said. 'It's urgent.'

The man in the black pants rubbed a hand over his bristled chin. It produced a scraping noise.

'Say, what the hell do you think you are? The Song of the Dawn? She don't receive visitors at this time. In fact, she don't receive visitors at any time unless they've fixed the date.'

Tearle thought that this wasn't one of the old school of servants. He lacked polish. But maybe he was something more than a servant. That would apply to all the staff in the house. They'd be a branch of the mob, as well.

'She'll see me. Just take me to her room.'

Black pants felt in his mouth. He took out a dental plate of four teeth. He wasn't risking those. Then he closed up on Tearle. He looked mean.

'You heard me the first time and I haven't changed my mind since then. I don't know you and I don't like you. Do you move all by yourself, or do I have to help you?'

This wasn't working out so well. Tearle didn't want any muscle play right now. That'd be sure to bring along the rest of the boys. He wanted to see Tina first — and alone.

Tearle worked up a grin.

'Take it easy. When I said it was urgent I wasn't kiddin' any. She'll see me and be glad. Tell her Tearle's here.'

His unshaven jaw went slack,

'Say . . . you're the guy who was in here before. The guy who . . . '

'That's me. But I'm playing ball with you boys this time. Just tell Tina I'm here.'

He still seemed uncertain. But he

shuffled off. Tearle let him move a few paces, then he followed.

They went up a curved staircase. Then along a wide corridor to a room near the end. As he paused to knock, black pants saw that Tearle was there.

'Hell! You seem to be sure of your reception,' he told him.

'I'll be okay.'

It took quite a lot of knocking before Tina's voice answered. Tearle gripped the door handle. He said: 'I'll take over from here.'

Then he pushed open the door of Tina's bedroom.

The curtains were drawn and the room was in a half-light: But he saw her clearly enough. She was lying back in the centre of the bed. A bed with a pink quilted headpiece. The sheets were pink, too. There was a faint aroma of her perfume in the place.

She sat up suddenly when she saw Tearle. And she looked okay, but very white. Her face, without make-up, was like new milk. It showed up that dark hair which hung on to her shoulders.

Tearle moved up to the side of the bed.

She said in an urgent kind of a whisper: 'You! What are you doing here? I heard you were trying to beat it outa town.'

'I was doing just that,' Tearle told her. 'And a whole lot's happened that you don't know about yet. I figure Ivan must be delaying telling you because maybe he was exceeding your orders . . . I'm here because I want to accept that offer about working in with you. Maybe there could be a big future in it.'

Her body went tense. Her oval eyes were fixed on him. They were hard, calculating.

'You sure can change your mind. I thought maybe you'd come round to that way of thinking when you realized how I'd got you and the whole of this burgh trussed up. But I didn't expect it at this time of the morning.'

Tearle worked up a tired grin.

'If you'll listen to me you'll understand a whole lot.'

He gave himself a second's pause. He needed it to get set for the biggest lie. All the time Tina was watching him.

110

Watching him in a way that made Tearle realise again that this wasn't going to be easy.

He said smoothly: 'I'm gonna come clean with you. It's the only way. I tried to give Ivan and a couple more of your guys the slip, so I made it fast for Frisco's Club. There I rang up a bud of mine on the *Tribune*. Then your boys came up. We shot it out. One of them, Aarga, had a serious kinda accident. Just before he was handed his harp he told me about the Western Allied Bank . . .'

She stood up suddenly and pulled a dressing gown over her. Her voice came in a taut whisper.

'Aarga told you!'

'Yeah. He was sore because the other boys left him in the desert to die. He gave me the whole set-up. With Cullen in on it, I guess it's just about foolproof.'

She was sitting on a chair now, still watching him.

'I'm listening. Go on.'

'I figured I'd be dumb to cut myself out of that sorta pitch. You said it'd pay me big to work for you. You told me you were planning to buy up a newspaper some-where. I didn't take a lot of notice because I didn't figure it was possible for you to lay your mitts on that kinda dough. I know you can now. And I know it'll be easy. That's why I'm here. If your offer still goes, I'm in on it.'

She sat very still for a long time. Just watching him. Once her lips parted as though she was going to speak. But she changed her mind.

When at last she did talk, she said: 'That friend you phoned who is on the *Tribune* . . . what did you tell him?'

'He was too scared to come, anyway. But when I knew the set-up I phoned him again. I told him I was okay and to forget about it. He sounded relieved. I guess he thinks I'm a bit crazy.'

'I guess he does. Give me a cigarette. We're gonna talk a lot . . . '

9

Looking for a Shroud

It was a long cross-examination. Tina didn't spare him any. But during it Tearle became more confident. The best way to tell a lie is to mix it up with a big measure of truth. That was what he did. In the end, Tina seemed to be convinced.

Then Tearle said: 'Now I'd like the whole pitch for today. Where do we go after the bank haul?'

She was sitting in front of her dressing table, busy with paint and powder. At first she didn't answer. Just went on applying the cosmetics. Examining herself critically. Then she put down a stick of rouge and turned towards him, like she'd come to a decision.

'Okay. You want to know and you'll have it your way. I guess you wouldn't have come here unless you were on the level.'

She turned back to her make-up.

While the work was going on she told him: 'Cullen's gonna call all cops off that beat at around midday. He's gonna have them working somewhere else on a phony. Then we're gonna move in on the bank. We're using two cars and they're fast, but even that ain't altogether necessary because there won't be any road chase. Cullen's gonna see to that, too. We'll be heading out on the east road. When we're well clear of this burgh there's gonna be a split up of the dough. Then we'll all go our own ways. But you and me — we'll go together.'

Tearle dragged deep on his cigarette. It wasn't tasting so good. That smell of old hay again.

He asked: 'Where does Cullen come in for his cut?'

'He'll be following us out. He'll be right behind us. He's leaving headquarters just as soon as he's been able to gum up any chance of a chase.'

Tearle said: 'He must be a trusting sorta bum. How does he know we'll wait for him?'

In the mirror Tearle saw her lips part in that humourless smile.

'He'll be paid off, because until he collects the dough he could make things awkward. But that doesn't go for the other boys. Not for Ivan and Pretty and Hal. Ivan and Pretty don't deserve any dough. They worked against my orders last night. Hal's dumb anyway and he wouldn't know what to do with it. That trio'll be happier without the stuff.'

'Yeah,' Tearle said. 'And just how are you gonna persuade them into thinking that way?'

She was drawing a thin line of rouge over the edges of her lips as she said: 'They're gonna get a spray of lead from a Thompson automatic gun. And you're the guy who'll use that gun . . . '

★ ★ ★

Ivan was feeling raw. Like his nerves had been scraped with rust. There was a lot on his mind. Tearle was on his mind. And Tina. And the coming bank snatch. Somehow he didn't feel so confident about any of them.

Tearle for instance. That punk reporter had got away clean. He could make a whole lot of trouble between now and midday. After midday it didn't matter. Not once they'd shared out the dough from the bank, Even now, he could be shooting his mouth off somewhere. And someone might be listening. Tina was crazy to ever have let him go from the city. But he knew why she'd done that. Ivan got around. He knew when a girl took a fancy to a guy. Tina sure liked Tearle. And folks don't break something they want. Not if there's any other way they don't.

Tina . . . Maybe she could be a bigger worry than Tearle. She didn't know yet that they'd tried to slay Tearle. But she'd have to know. That would be uncovered when she found that Aarga wasn't around.

Ivan figured he'd be able to settle Tina okay after they'd got the dough. But that wasn't yet. Not for another couple of hours or more.

He didn't want to break with Tina before then. Without her, they'd never get out of that bank. Might not even get into it. It was Tina who was working in with Cullen. And it was Cullen who was making it possible. If that cop thought Tina'd been two-timed he'd most likely reverse his tactics and have them shot down just as soon as they got near the bank.

Tina had a working arrangement with Cullen. It'd all been fixed between those two, since before the time it was planned to give the works to Daks. No, Cullen wouldn't play without Tina. So somehow Tina had to be calmed down when she learned about that shooting on the desert road.

And the bank snatch itself . . .

That ought to be a nursery ride. It didn't look like it could work out any other way while the chief of police was cooperating. There was only one guard in the Western Allied and they'd nail him okay. Yeah, it ought to be easy. And it ought to be easy to fix Tina when she made the share-out on the highway. She'd be alone after Cullen had gone. And he'd have Pretty and Hal with him. Sure, Tina was tough. But not all that tough. It ought to be easy . . .

But there was that doubt somewhere. Maybe it was just his nerves. Tina would be coming downstairs soon. When he'd got the interview about Aarga over he guessed he'd feel better.

He went to the cabinet and poured himself a deep drink. Then he started to think about that reporter. He'd like to know what he was doing.

Tearle leaned himself against the edge of the door and said to Ivan: 'Get one for me. Both of us had a busy night.'

Ivan had had his back to the door. He swivelled round on his heels, spilling most of the stuff in his glass. Some blotches appeared on his big pan. He looked like he'd just eaten something that always made him vomit.

Tearle repeated: 'I want a drink. I mean right now. Don't stand around trying to look decorative. That's wasting time.'

Ivan went on wasting time. His mouth opened in a slow and slack way, but he didn't talk. It seemed he wasn't in a conversational kind of mood.

This was getting no place. Tearle

detached himself from the door. He eased up to Ivan. He took what remained of the spilled drink. Ivan let it go without doing a thing.

'Thanks,' Tearle said. 'I guess I might as well use yours then I'll know it's okay.'

When he'd finished the whisky Ivan had recovered some of his power of conversation.

He said: 'Bud . . . you must be lookin' for a shroud.'

And he felt under his left shoulder.

Tearle moved fast and gripped his gun wrist while it was still under the coat.

'Don't start being noisy,' he said. 'Tina wouldn't like it. She's expecting us guys to get along good.'

A bulge bobbed up and down in the front of Ivan's throat.

When he spoke his tones came like the twanging of a frayed banjo string.

'Tina's expectin' that . . . '

'Yeah. I've just been talking to her. She said to go and make good friends with Ivan.'

Ivan twanged: 'Either you're crazy or she is . . . '

119

Tina came in.

She was in a linen dress. She looked cool. And she looked hard. She had a cigarette in that holder. She gave it level and steady to Ivan.

'There's only one thing crazy about me,' she told him. 'That's keeping a creep like you on in this outfit. But it's too late to make changes. Tearle's in with us. He's been late about it, but he's taken up my offer. He's a wise guy and he's joining up with the dough. And now we ain't got Aarga, we can use him.'

Ivan drew in a deep breath.

'He's been tellin' you about last night?'

'Sure. And it seems you didn't come out so smart.'

Ivan was still looking a bit dizzy. Tearle watched him. He watched him anxiously. He was wondering whether Ivan would remember that call he'd made to Dugan. He didn't want him to remember the details of that.

And Ivan said: 'You didn't look like you were gonna work in with us when . . . '

Tearle cut in fast.

'This ain't any time to hold inquests.

120

I've told it all to Tina and she's satisfied. I got wise to myself. That doesn't mean I've started to like you any, but I'm gonna work with you and you might as well accept that.'

Then Pretty and Hal came in.

If Ivan had been going to talk about the call to Dugan, he forgot about it now. It was quite a time before they got things right. Tina explained the pitch to them. They couldn't do a thing about it. But they were no more pleased than Ivan. And that meant they weren't pleased at all. Pretty in particular. Pretty knew Tina's angle on Tearle. He wasn't so dumb. He didn't like her fancy for this news-bum. His pride was kind of hurt. And Pretty had plenty of pride. So it was often getting hurt.

Tina finished the talk when she looked at her gold and diamond watch and said: 'We move out of here at fifteen minutes to twelve. That ought to bring us at the bank dead on midday. Which means we've a couple of hours to relax in. I'm gonna relax right here in this room. There's only one guy I want around while I'm doing it.'

They understood. They got out. But on the way, they gave Tearle some mean looks.

Tina sat herself in the settee. Tearle got right beside her. After a while he said: 'That kid Farrel. You said he wouldn't burn. Is that right?'

It was a soft lead up and Tina laughed.

'You still interested in that hick? Say, you oughta open a children's farm.'

'It ain't charity that makes me ask. I'm just curious.'

She fitted a new cigarette in the holder. Then she said: 'Cullen and me fixed this bank deal a long time back. But Daks wouldn't have any part of it. Just refused to play. Said he'd plenty of dough operating his organisation in Vallis City. And he liked Vallis City. Didn't want to have to quit it for the sake of dough he didn't need.'

Tearle nodded. He was grinning. It wasn't a pleasant kind of grin. But Tina wasn't looking at him. Which could have been fortunate.

'So you decided to get rid of Daks — you and Cullen. And to make it look a real smooth job you framed this kid.'

Tina was pleased at the recollection.

She told him: 'That's the way it was. And we played it neat. This hick had come into the city from up-country looking for work. He was just what was needed. I found him and I worked on him. He fell okay. I took him in that night and gave him a drink while Ivan saw to Daks. As soon as Daks was out of the way I gave him a lot of dough and told him to get out quick. Cullen did the rest of the work. By making a show of searching for him he made it look more convincing. But he got a bit worried when Suzette slipped him the mickey finn. He thought he might have lost him.

'But it was okay. The citizenry got their arrest — which was all they wanted. It don't matter if a guy's not guilty, just so long as there's an arrest.'

Tearle said: 'Then Farrel will be okay after Cullen beats it. He'll have to be freed for want of evidence.'

Tina said she guessed so. But she wasn't interested in Farrel.

After a while Tearle told her: 'I'm

gonna take some air in the garden.'

She was combing out her jet hair.

'We ain't got so long now.'

'I won't be so long. But I haven't had any sleep. A walk'll clear my head.'

She didn't seem to mind at all as he eased out of the house.

Tearle walked around the lawns for a few minutes. He did it in an obvious way for the benefit of Ivan. Ivan was watching him from a ground floor window. So was Hal. Hal's pan could be seen over Ivan's shoulder. Tearle was just as obvious about his walk back to the house.

He looked in the lounge. It was empty. Tina must have gone upstairs. He glanced back into the hall. That was empty, too. Then he shut the door. He'd like to have locked it, but that would have been playing too safe.

Then he crossed to the phone. He was sweating when he picked it up and said to the operator: 'Get me the Western Allied Bank.'

He said it so soft that the operator asked him to come again. Tearle glanced at the door. It was still tight shut. He repeated. This time the operator heard.

It seemed to take one hell of a time before the call was put through. That was because the operator had to find the number.

At last a voice said: 'Western Allied Bank.'

Tearle's lips were almost pressing into the receiver.

'Get me through to the president's office. It's urgent,' he hissed.

The man at the other end said he'd do that.

More waiting. More hard sweating.

Then came the sound. It was a sound he didn't want to hear. But you just could not mistake it.

Which meant that someone had lifted an extension phone and had started to listen. Tearle thought fast. He couldn't end the call. If he replaced his own receiver the guy on the extension would still be able to hear the bank president come through And it'd be easy work for him to find out who the call had been made to. After that it'd be twilight for Tearle.

There was a cough at the bank end of the wire. Someone was about to talk. But Tearle talked first

He said: 'Hello — that the Central Garage Corporation?'

The boy with the cough sounded surprised and maybe a bit sore.

'It's not,' he said. 'This is . . . '

'Gee, I sure am sorry,' Tearle cut in. 'I musta got on to the wrong number.'

He waited for the phone to be replaced at the bank end. Then he called the operator again.

'I haven't a directory manual here,' he told the operator. It was a different operator from the last time. 'I've just got a number mixed. Get me through to the Central Garage Corporation.'

Tearle was feeling a bit easier now. He did business with that firm. Genuine business. He figured he could put himself in the clear with whoever was listening.

When the garage answered, he said: 'This is Tearle here. I'd fixed to turn in my coupé in tonight for servicing. But I've got to go away on sudden business. I thought maybe you'd better know.'

The garage thanked him. They said they'd be pleased to check over his car at any time.

He pushed away the phone and slumped into a chair. He felt kind of weak. Like he'd spent too long in a too hot bath. He'd covered himself okay. But he gave thanks to his star of destiny that the person who'd picked up the extension hadn't done so just half a minute later. Then he'd have been talking to the bank president. Giving him an anonymous tip-off.

Tearle remembered the drinks cabinet. He dispensed himself a rye and after it he felt stronger. He figured that the call might have done him some good. It would confirm to whoever was snooping that he was serious. Anyway, it would seem to confirm that. But he still hadn't been able to do anything for those people in the bank. Tearle wasn't the squeamish kind. Not particularly. But he didn't like to think of what could happen when the mob moved in on to the bank premises. Any show of resistance and there would be slaughter.

The Western Allied was not a big bank, although it did a lot of business in Vallis City. The total staff was no more than a dozen. Tearle had been in it a few times. It was the sort of place that makes you feel like you've entered a museum. All silence and dignity. There wouldn't be either when the mob got to work.

He started to think about his own chances of surviving the day. He wasn't encouraged by the prospects. He wondered why the hell he'd not kept clear of it all. And he found he couldn't answer that. Anyway he couldn't answer it logically. Farrel had something to do with it. A lot, perhaps But it wasn't only Farrel. Maybe it was because he didn't like being pushed around. And until that mob was fixed, he wasn't going to prosper any. He'd been nicely framed himself. Farrel was the only one to complain. He'd been framed right from the time Hyman had been told he was to be charged with assault. That meant more than losing one job. With that sort of charge hanging over him, he wasn't going to find it easy to find another. No editor likes to employ reporters who go around slugging women. Even women like Tina.

As he drained his glass he thought some more about Tina.

Then she came in. She had a hat on now and she was holding a big leather despatch case. It wasn't hard to figure out what it was intended for. She looked kind of extra pleased.

'Fix me a drink, honey,' she told Tearle. 'We move in five minutes.'

Tearle had half forgotten the time. Five minutes. As close as that.

He fixed her drink. She took it and said: 'You won't be using your car, anyway. We need big saloons for this kinda work. Still, it was nice of you to let the garage know. I go for that sorta consideration.'

He tried to look surprised. Part of that look was genuine. In the back of his mind he always had a hunch that Ivan had been doing the phone snoop.

'You listened? Hell, you sure do keep tapes on me.'

She stroked his chin.

'Relax. I just happened to pick up the

phone at the time. That was all. There was nothin' to it. But it makes me still more sure that I've got a right guy. We're goin' places when today's work's over.'

Tearle agreed that they were going places. They finished the drinks. Tina said: 'I'm travelling with you in the front car. Hal will be driving. Ivan and Pretty'll be right behind us. All you've gotta do is stick around with me. Ivan'll see to most of the arm work.'

Ivan eased through the door. He acted as if Tearle wasn't there.

'We're all set,' he said. 'The cars are waiting.'

Tearle saw that Ivan and Pretty's saloon was being driven by black pants — the bum he'd met in the kitchen. Black pants was wearing a chauffeur's uniform. So was Hal.

They rolled down the drive, en route for the Western Allied Bank.

Tina glanced at Tearle. She smiled. It was an understanding smile. She told him: 'Take it easy. Sit back and relax. I guess you ain't used to this sorta thing, but you'll see the attraction in it soon.

There's not a thing to worry about. Not with Cullen fixing the cops.'

He tried to give her a confident smile. It didn't look so confident. Hard thoughts were circulating in his brain. He was figuring that Dugan was the only guy who could clear him of this. If anything happened to Dugan, or if no one listened to Dugan, then the law would believe that he'd properly changed his mind. He'd be wanted as a bank breaker. As a killer, too. He'd killed Aarga. And Tina'd booked him to slay the rest of the boys when this bit of business was done.

The hour had been chosen well. Vallis City, being a hot place, relaxed at midday and didn't start to move again at full pitch until around three o'clock. The streets weren't deserted. But they were quiet.

The Western Allied Bank was slightly off the main street on a secondary avenue. That made the locality extra quiet. It was a big stone building set on a corner. Hal braked just short of that corner and stayed in the driving seat. The other car stopped a few yards behind them.

131

Tina said: 'Now relax and look natural. This is gonna be a pushover, but we need that bit of a surprise. Just stick with me like I said. The other boys know what to do.'

They got out on to the sidewalk. There was no more than a dozen folks in sight along the whole length of the avenue.

Ivan and Pretty walked slowly past them. They gave no sign of recognition. They might have been strangers to each other. Each of the pair had a weathercoat draped over an arm. Like they were expecting a cloudburst.

Tina's eyes were hard as she watched them get level with the bank entrance.

'Okay,' she said. 'This is where we follow. I got a gun for you, but I'm not counting on you needin' it.'

She felt in a flap of the despatch case.

'It ain't necessary,' Tearle told her, patting his jacket pocket. 'I'm carrying my own artillery.'

They were walking as she said: 'My Derringer?'

'Not on your life. A Colt. A Derringer's a toy.'

They pushed through the glass swing doors of the bank. It was a long place, with the counter running the whole length. A half-dozen clerks were behind it. Behind the clerks was a glass partition that concealed the rest of the staff.

There were no customers about.

Ivan and Pretty had split. Ivan was talking to the clerk nearest the door. Pretty was doing the same thing to the guy at the far end. They were making enquiries about opening an account.

The bank guard was sitting on a stool a few yards from the door. He wasn't taking a lot of interest in anything. His head was slumped forward and he looked like he would go to sleep at any moment. That was the way hot weather got the elderly in sedentary occupations. Occupations in which the same thing happens every day. And that's nothing. Anyway, nothing until today.

Tina gave the signal.

She tapped one of her high heels hard on the marble floor.

The boys went into action.

10

No Gold for Tina

When Tina said the boys knew what to do she hadn't been kidding anyone. Ivan and Hal moved with the sort of timing you'd expect from U.S. marines.

In the same second, they dropped their weathercoats and a short Thompson gun was tucked under each of their arms. The barrels of those Thompsons had been sawn off eighteen inches from the breech. This made them easy to handle. It spoiled their accuracy, but accuracy wasn't so important in this kind of work. No one and nothing could miss at a maximum range of a few feet.

The guns were levelled across the cash counter.

Ivan said: 'Stand right where you are. Don't let any guy so much as sneeze. We ain't here on a social call.'

The clerks did just as he said. Not

altogether because they were scared. The scared feeling was due to come a bit later. They were still because they were plain surprised. They'd read in the newspapers about this kind of thing happening. They'd wondered what they'd do if it ever happened in their bank. But none of them had ever figured that it really would happen like this. They gaped blankly at the tommy guns.

Pretty moved towards the counter flap, lifted it, then went behind the partition. He was going to handle the rest of the staff.

Tina hadn't been idle. Tina wasn't an idle sort of girl. Immediately after she'd given the signal she closed up to the guard. The guard was still on the brink of sleep. Maybe his eyelids weren't completely closed. But they weren't open, either. But he didn't remain in that state of compromise for long Tina settled the matter for him. She had a gun in her gloved hand. Not a Derringer this time. Something a whole lot bigger. She moved her arm in a wide arc. The butt of the weapon slapped against the side of the guard's skull, at a point just above the ear.

His next important journey could be in a hearse.

The guard started to roll forward off his chair. Tina caught him. She held him before he hit the floor, but with difficulty. He wasn't a fragile kind of man.

She said to Tearle: 'Take him and prop him in the chair. Make him look nice and natural.'

Tearle took the weight from her. His brain was in high gear as he got the guard fixed in the chair.

Tina had crossed the floor and was behind the counter. She was talking to one of the clerks. And she was making her meaning clear by pressing the barrel of her gun in the centre of his belly. The clerk was one of those men who wear thick horn glasses. All intellect and astigmatism. He was blinking at her. His eyes were wet and they were making his glasses steam. And his face . . . his face was the colour of bad cheese.

★　★　★

She was saying: 'Gimme the deposit box keys in the name of Daks Dygen . . . and I hope you haven't forgotten where they are, because if that happens to be so you're in for a rough time.'

The clerk remembered where they were. He pulled open a drawer. Then he handed a couple of small keys to Tina.

They rattled together with the shake of his hand.

She took them from him. Her hands weren't shaking. Then she said: 'You're doin' fine, brother. Now take me right to the deposit boxes . . .'

He swayed down to the far end, where an open steel door showed into the strong room.

Tearle watched and his eyes got narrow.

He thought: 'I must be smart. This is the second hunch that's come up right. Daks' dough was locked in a private deposit box in here. Even after he died, she couldn't get the keys because they are kept right here and only Daks would have authority to open it. So that's another nice reason for the stick-up. So she can get in among Daks' personal dough . . .'

He figured that Daks' money was likely to be small denomination bills. Which was good for Tina. But a lot of the bank's float would be held in big value currency, which could be traced. So the mob couldn't snatch all they saw in the bank. That made Daks' bullion extra important.

There came the distant sound of a motor horn. And that was the only sound that broke the stillness in the bank. It seemed to come from some remote world. It was as though nothing outside could have any connection with this place. This place which held two sorts of people. Frightened people and desperate people.

Tearle made his decision. It had to be done and this looked like it was as good a time as any. No one was watching him.

Hal and black pants were outside in the cars. Tina was being taken into the strong room. The staff was under the concentrated gaze of Ivan and Pretty . . .

Tearle eased through the counter flap and went behind the glass partition. Pretty was there. Pretty was holding his

Thompson like he was itching to use it. The butt was pressed against his ribs and his trigger finger was coiled and taut. In front of him were nine or ten scared people sitting behind desks. That was the only difference between them and the staff behind the counter. This bunch was sitting. The others were standing.

An open door showed off into a salubrious kind of office. But Tearle could see that the office was empty. On the door there was a notice that said it should be occupied by the bank president. Pretty had been in there and had got the president out. He was now sitting with the rest of his staff.

Pretty gave Tearle a fast glance. Just for a split moment. Then he looked back at the people in front of his gun.

He said: 'I don't need help. Not from amateurs. If you wanta be useful, tell Tina I'm gettin' tired of waiting. I want to see that dough.'

'Tina's getting the dough,' Tearle told him. 'She's operating in the strongroom right now.'

He'd eased up to Pretty. So he was

standing slightly behind him. He calculated the exact spot on the back of Pretty's fair head. The spot where the gun-butt would send him out quick and quiet.

He had to be goddammed careful about that. If he hit the wrong place, then Pretty's finger would instinctively contract over the trigger and the morticians would be making a sweet turnover. It had to hit a place where the blackout was instantaneous.

Maybe he hesitated too long. Maybe he was trying to be that bit too careful.

He was still balancing the barrel of the Colt in his hand when Pretty glanced over his shoulder.

Pretty breathed: 'You double-crossing — ' and he tried to twist away from the gun-butt.

It missed his head. It came down on the edge of his left shoulder blade. Pretty gave out a groan. His pan became pallid with pain. But he swung the automatic gun towards Tearle's belly. Appearances can be deceptive. Pretty was tough. But not tough enough. That pain in his shoulder was making him hold the gun too low. Tearle grabbed the end of the barrel with one hand and forced it down so it was aimed at the floor.

It was then that Pretty squeezed on the trigger. The floor was of marble here, too. And .300 slugs don't go through that sort of material. The stream of lead knocked away flinty chunks and richochetted against the wall. Half the magazine must have been emptied that way before Pretty let go the trigger.

In the sudden silence there was only the heavy breathing of the two men who swayed against each other.

They didn't sway for long. Hal was under orders to come in if things seemed to be going wrong. He was likely to come in now. It was important to get Pretty out of the way fast.

Tearle was still holding the Colt by the barrel. He brought it up so that the steel underpart of the butt slapped against the edge of Pretty's jaw.

Pretty wasn't due to make any more friends or influence any more people for quite a while.

Tearle got his gun. The breech was hot and it smelled of cordite.

The guys behind the desks hadn't moved. Tearle saw that they were watching him in just the same way as they'd watched Pretty. In unbelieving horror. It'd be optimistic to expect much help from them. Or that was the way it seemed to him.

But he was wrong.

An elderly man with a lot of thick, white hair got up from behind one of the desks. He was bewildered. Obviously, he couldn't figure out who Tearle was or what he was attempting to do. Tearle thought: 'This could be the bank president.'

As he moved down the side of the partition in the direction of the strong-room, Tearle gave him a quick nod. The old guy understood. He was shaking. But he followed. And one or two of the clerks were standing now. They were taking up the lead given by the boss.

The strongroom was concealed by a small swing door at the bottom end. Tearle pushed it open. The president was close behind him.

Tina hadn't let the shooting distract her any. She must have figured that Pretty was taking care of some awkward boy Right now, she was standing just outside the open strongroom door. The petrified clerk was passing her thick wads of bills from out of a steel box. This was Daks' dough. She was due to collect the bank's float when this was secure. That would mean going through the counter drawers. Most of the money in the strongroom would be in the big denominations.

Tina looked up at Tearle. She seemed a bit surprised. But she went on stuffing some money into the despatch case as she said: 'What happened way up back?'

Tearle said: 'Plenty. Pretty's kinda hurt.'

The clerk was going back into the strongroom. He'd never worked so fast before. He found the gun still in Tina's right hand to be a spur to industry.

Tina said: 'How come? These slobs seem tame to me.'

'It wasn't one of these slobs,' Tearle told her softly. 'It was me. Honey, I've decided that crime just don't pay . . . '

She took a step away from the despatch case. And she looked at the Thompson. It was aimed at her. Aimed steady on her. The fury of the ages gathered up in Tina's eyes.

It was not much more than a whisper. But a whisper was enough. She said: 'You two-timin' . . . '

The bank president started moving. He'd got his nerve back now. He made a rush at the strongroom door as the clerk was emerging. He snatched the dough from the clerk, threw it inside, then slammed the steel door shut.

In the centre of the big panel there was a combination dial. His hand went up to turn that dial and so send home the internal locks. It quivered and paused on the dial. His hand did that for a good reason.

A slice had been torn out of his chest.

It happened like that. The sound and the realisation that Ivan had opened up from his position at the counter seemed to come after the effect was visible. A short burst of slugs.

It could be that he was already dead when he did it. Maybe it was a muscular reaction. But his hand turned the dial a fraction of an inch. That was all. Just a fraction. But it was enough to secure the door.

Now there was a new sound. The sound of shouting outside in the street. The shooting had been heard.

Tearle saw Tina — and he saw the purest concentration of hell.

But he had to forget about Tina. There was a movement behind him. It was Hal.

Hal had his gun out. But he was holding it in a clumsy way. He wasn't sure what to do with it. He was trying to figure what was going on. It was because Hal was dumb that he'd been kept out of the way unless there was an emergency. Tearle turned to meet him. He knew what was likely to happen as he did it. But there was no option about it. He had to turn his back on Tina.

And Ivan, too. Ivan was coming up.

As he grabbed for Hal's gun, Tearle heard Tina hiss: 'We gotta shoot our way outa here. But don't shoot him. I want him all to myself . . . '

Tearle got hold of Hal's gun. He forced the barrel down. But that was only because Hal wasn't worrying so much about his artillery. Tina had said not to shoot.

Hal suddenly released the gun. Then he closed in on Tearle.

There was a brief moment while Tearle gathered himself.

His right mitt travelled towards the hoodlum's jaw. It moved so fast it could be seen only as a pink blur. And when it landed Tearle felt a shock streak up the length of his arm. It had been a near-perfect effort. But Hal only stepped back a half pace and shook his head. Tearle cursed mentally. He thought: 'You're losing your nerve. That's the wrong place to hit that sort of bum. Their pans are made of concrete. You should have gone for his middle . . . '

Hal's arms came out. They extended like those of a maddened chimp. They closed round Tearle before he could move away. This was Hal's favourite method. The method by which he could use his

146

muscle power to squeeze a man into unconsciousness. He was using that method now.

He pulled Tearle close to him. Then he contracted his arms. Tearle tried to force himself away. That was hopeless. Tearle was no weakling. Nobody had ever worried about him going into a decline. But he could do just nothing against this strength. And he couldn't breathe properly.

He tried to draw a foot back to kick. That was as far as he got. He drew his foot back. It didn't thrust forward.

Something exploded against the back of his skull.

Hal's pan shrunk to pinpoint size. Then it disappeared into a purple mist.

11

A Cop Collects

There was not much that Tearle could look at when he finally woke up. Not while he was lying on the floor at the back of the car. But he could see Tina. Tina was on the seat. Anyway, she was all he could see unless he chose to move. Tearle could do that. But not much. Not enough. His wrists had been lashed behind his back. With his own necktie.

Judging by the pitch of the engine, the saloon was making fast going.

He twisted his head. That head felt sore again. And sticky. That'd be dry blood. Tina was alone on the seat. Her gun was in her hand. And there was something odd about the way she looked. A desperate intensity. Her lips were no longer full. They were drawn tight. So was her skin. Somehow she was no longer such a glamour puss.

She glanced down at Tearle. Her eyes still smouldered. She said: 'You're gonna die, Mister Tearle. I'm gonna make you die. You're gonna scream first.'

He managed to get himself into an upright sitting position. He didn't want to answer her. There was nothing to say. Nothing that could make any difference.

She put out a foot. A foot in a pointed shoe. The point hit him over an eye. He was knocked back flat on the floor. He decided to stay like that.

But the engine was beginning to slow. Presently the saloon braked to a stop. Ivan came along from out of the other car. It'd been right behind.

Ivan opened the door and he said to Tina: 'We don't have to wait for him. We got no dough for him, so let me fix this newshawk then we can beat it fast.'

Tina got out. She stood on the road and sized up to Ivan.

'We gotta wait for Cullen. If he thinks we've double-crossed him he can still get the law on our tail. He ain't done nothing yet that he can't wriggle out of. He hasn't accepted any dough and he's not going to because there ain't any — so he's in the clear. Nothing can be proved against Cullen. But he could still make us roast.'

Ivan thought for a while. Then he said maybe she was right. Tearle decided he might as well take it easy. He pushed himself on to the vacant seat. From there he could see most that mattered. The saloon was parked on a grass verge at the side of a secondary highway. A poor secondary highway by the look of it. One that was not much used. It was narrow and the surface was rough.

Through the back glass he could see into the other car. Black pants was sitting at the wheel. He looked pretty sick. Like the rest of the mob. Especially Pretty. Pretty was right beside the driving seat. And he was holding his broken jaw. Maybe they'd have to find another name for that bum.

A third car was coming up. Tearle watched it. It was moving fast and when it got near it braked hard, like time was important. Cullen got out.

There was a lot of sweat on Cullen's pan. His pipe was between his teeth, but it wasn't lighted and the bowl was upside down. But he looked like he didn't care. He walked fast up to Tina.

'What the hell happened?' he rasped. 'I got reports that there was shooting and you had to force your way out.'

Tina's lips warped into a curl. She indicated the inside of the car with a jerk of her head.

'He was in with us. Only his nerve broke. He decided to work in the interests of the bank. He gave one of the guys time to lock the safe.'

Cullen was breathing as if he'd just finished a long run.

But there was something ominously level about his voice when he asked if they'd cleared any dough.

Tina was looking straight at him when she said: 'A thousand bucks.'

There was a long silence. Cullen broke it.

'A thousand . . . And this was gonna be a million-dollar snatch . . . '

He spat on the road.

'You're all washed up. Tina. Your whole outfit's washed up. And I figured you were smart. I thought that with my cooperation this job'd set a new high on bank jobs. Luxury for all of us. But you manage to ball it up because some . . . '

He moved nearer the car and looked inside. His mouth dropped slack when he saw Tearle. Cullen was having a bad day.

'That's the bum you ran outa town. What the devil . . . ?'

Ivan came in. He started to sing strong. 'She took a fancy to him. So she falls when he comes along with a nice line about wanting to work in with us.'

Cullen said: 'You bitch. You gummed this up because — Well, I ain't gonna suffer because of you. I'm in the clear. Those cops were called away from the bank area by mistake you hear? I'm putting out a call and I'm having every road blocked so the patrolmen'll pick you up inside of a couple of hours. I'm turning this set-up so it can do me some good. It'll sound fine when the citizens hear how I chased out after you alone and picked up your trail. Maybe I'm a bit sorry. But you've flopped and from now on I gotta play my own way.'

Tearle had eased himself out of the saloon and was now standing on the road. It had been a difficult operation, but he'd done it. He managed to work on a grin as he spoke to Cullen.

'Where do I come into the set-up?'

Cullen pulled out his pipe.

'Where d'yer think? You threw in with the mob.'

Tearle was still grinning when he said: 'That won't ring out so clear. At least a dozen guys in that bank saw me have a bit of an argument with the mob. In fact, Tina's just told you how I gummed the works. You won't be able to laugh off that testimony. You'll have an interesting time answering the questions that are going to come about me.'

Cullen rubbed his chin. Tina said: 'Captain Cullen's gonna have an interesting time right now. He's gonna step slap into the scroll of eternity.'

Cullen turned quickly towards her. Tina's gun was on him. By the way she held it, he knew she was talking serious business. His pan started to lose colour.

'Say, Tina, don't go plumb crazy. You

can't use that on me.'

She said: 'You're making a big mistake, cop. I can. We're gettin' right outa here. But we won't do it while you're breathing.'

A deep flow of sweat started down Cullen's cheeks.

'You're gettin' it all wrong. I guess we're all of us strung up. Let's see if we can figure another way out.'

Tina laughed. An ill-tuned laugh.

'I've done my figuring. You ain't turning us in. Look around you. Look at the sun. You won't see it again . . . '

Cullen broke. Or maybe it'd be better to say he snapped.

He started to whimper like a kid.

'Don't do this to me, Tina . . . you can't . . . '

She still was wearing that twisted smile.

And she said: 'Maybe I won't if you ask nicely. I've never had much respect from cops. Even crooked cops. Do your pleading in a proper way. *Get down on you knees, punk!*'

Cullen opened his mouth. He wanted to scream. But he couldn't scream. Only a weak croak came out from his paralysed throat.

Tina pressed the trigger.

The gun jerked in her gloved hand.

Tina said: 'Put him in the ditch. He'll rest quiet there for a long time.'

Ivan and Hal picked him up. They threw him into a roadside drainage furrow.

Ivan said: 'Now we gotta move fast.' He glanced at Tearle. 'Let me fix this slob like I said. Then we can split that thousand bucks and beat it for the border.'

Tina rubbed the stem of the cigarette holder against her sharp teeth. There was something final about it when she said: 'We're not beating it across any border.'

Ivan absorbed the information.

'Yeah . . . d'yer wanta hang around here until the Feds come up? This area's hot now. There'll be a Federal investigation.'

'Sure.' Tina told him. 'And we can't get over the border without being seen. And now we have no real dough we can't get far. We'd be hauled back. We're gonna hang out at a little place I know just five miles from here until the heat cools off.'

Ivan didn't look so sure

He said: 'I don't know of any place.'

'Maybe. But that don't impress me any. We'll be okay where I'm taking you. Okay for months. Let's go.'

On the way back to the cars she said to Hal: 'Follow this road along then take the left turn up the hill track. It's rough going, but we can make it.'

Before getting behind the wheel Hal pushed Tearle into the back of the saloon. He was on the floor again. Tina didn't even look at him as she settled herself on the seat.

12

Cremation

When Hal saw it he said: 'Aw, this is one helluva dump!'

Tina said: 'Keep goin'. It's gotta do.'

But Hal was right. It wasn't much more than a shack A long time ago (a very long time ago), used by a prospector who figured there might be gold seams in the rocks. He'd figured wrong. The place had never been occupied since — not permanently.

Inside there was still some furniture. A bare wood table. A few chairs. But that was all. The two rooms smelled of dust and decay. Even the rats had deserted it.

Ivan still wasn't pleased as they looked around.

'We gotta eat,' he said. 'We gotta have something to cook with.'

'You're gonna fix that right now,' Tina told him. 'There's a small town on the

157

other side of the valley about ten miles off. But don't go right there. You can approach it by the east road and take the same road back. That way, the residents won't know where you came from or are goin' to.'

Ivan nodded. Then he remembered Cullen's car. Pretty had managed to bring that car along. Now he was slumped on a hard chair. He looked like he was running to a fever.

'What are we gonna do about Cullen's auto? I don't like keepin' it here.'

Tina said: 'Leave that kinda worrying to me. That car ain't hot. It ain't a cop car. Cullen was figurin' on using that to make the pace across the border with his cut of the dough. Now get goin' and come back with the comforts.'

Ivan eased out. Hal looked at Tearle then at Tina.

'Are yer gonna fix him now?' he asked.

Tina said: 'Tonight. After we've got this place in shape. Then we're gonna have some fun with that Romeo.'

★ ★ ★

Ivan was back when it was starting to get dark. He came with a big supply of provisions. Most of it was in tins. He brought a pressure stove, too, and a can of paraffin oil. Hal knew how to rustle up a meal. He got busy. There was an iron range in a corner of the shack that burned wood. But they didn't want to use that in case the smoke was seen.

Tearle hadn't enjoyed the interval. His hands were still lashed with the necktie. He'd been pushed into a corner where he sat amongst the grime on the floor. He was getting tired of sitting on floors. He figured a chair would make a nice change.

Tina went on ignoring him. She ignored him when they got down to plates of ham and eggs. He wasn't offered any of that. And neither was Pretty. But Pretty didn't want to eat. They found an old mattress and stretched him on it. He was getting delirious.

It was when they'd finished eating that Tina lighted a cigarette, pushed back her chair, and looked at Tearle in a reflective kind of way.

She said to Ivan: 'How long do you

think we can make that punk last?'

Ivan thought he'd last a long time. Hours, maybe. With that sort of physique he'd stand a lot of treatment.

Tina gave out that smile. The smile without humour.

Ivan crushed out his own cigarette. Tina went over to the pressure stove and turned the flame so it roared. She put the blade of an eating-knife into it. Almost immediately the steel went red then changed to white. It wasn't hard to figure out what she was going to do with that knife. His throat went dry and seemed to swell.

But now Ivan had got a hold of him. Using both hands, he dragged him upright. He ripped his jacket off, tearing up the back seam. There was a grin on Ivan's pan while he did it. But Tearle wasn't watching Ivan. His attention was concentrated on Tina.

He figured that this was the time to start playing his hand. There wasn't likely to be any other time.

Tearle backed a bit from Ivan.

He said to him: 'You've been a lucky

boy. It would have been tough for you if you'd got that dough.'

Ivan had been putting out a hand to tear off his shirt. The hand stayed outstretched — but motionless. He looked suddenly puzzled.

'It wouldn't have been any burden to me. But cease the cracks. We're gonna be mighty busy.'

Somehow, Tearle worked up a grin.

'You sure are right about it not being a burden. If you'd collected the bank money you'd have been cold meat by this hour.'

Through the corner of his eye he saw Tina straighten, leaving the knife in the flame.

Ivan said: 'Yer goin' crazy before yer time. Take it easy.'

But he was still standing still.

'I ain't crazy. You boys are the crazy section of this outfit. You must be dumb to trust Tina. She gave me the order to fill you guys with lead when we stopped to split up the dough. She was going to let Cullen have his split, then when he'd gone you were to have it.'

Tina had come up to them. Her mouth was in that tight line.

'He talks sweet,' she said. 'But it won't get him outa this place. The boys aren't that dumb. They know I don't organise deals like that.'

Ivan slowly turned his head and looked at her. She looked right back. Ivan said slowly: 'I ain't so sure. You were crazy about this guy. That'd be just the sorta thing you might do.'

Hal had closed up. He was listening.

Tina tried giving it to Ivan.

'Quit talking. We've got important work to do. Work that's gonna give me a whole lot of pleasure.'

Ivan gripped the front of Tearle's shirt. He was going to rip that, too. But he changed his mind. It was a nice kind of shirt. White silk. The sort that a guy like Ivan didn't often wear.

'I can use that,' Ivan muttered. He unfastened the necktie and Tearle's hands were free. But right now there was not a lot of use in them. They were cramped. Ivan pulled the shirt off his back while Tina and Hal looked on. But he was still thinking about what Tearle had told him. His brow was heavy with the effort of thinking.

Tearle said: 'She wanted me to use one of the automatic guns on you boys.'

Again Ivan became rigid. Tina started some action. She whipped an open palm across Tearle's face. There was some jewellery on her fingers and the blow cut his skin.

'Pipe down. No one's believing you. You ain't talking your way out of this.'

Hal eased in. Hal was a guy who didn't often get ideas.

But when he did, he held on to them. He'd got an idea right now.

'I believe him. It sure sounds like a right sorta story to me.'

'You're getting smart,' Tearle told Hal. 'She said to me that dough was no use to a dumb hood, anyway.'

The whites of Hal's eyes got larger.

'She said that about me?'

'Yeah. She said just that.'

Tina had her gun in her hand. It was aimed at Tearle's head. And she was going to send that slug over. That was her intention. But Hal interfered.

He grabbed the gun with a massive hand. A twist and he had it away from her.

He said: 'You don't wanta stop this guy from singin', do you, Tina? I'm findin' it mighty entertaining.'

Tina was tensed like a wild cat.

'Gimme back that gun. You ain't running this outfit . . . '

Ivan cut in: 'You're right, he ain't. But you ain't either. I figure I'm with Hal. I think this punk's given it out right. Yer through, sister. You and yer Romeo are gonna go out together. Truss her, Hal.'

Tina knew a whole lot of moves in the science of self-defence. Most of them were unorthodox. She used most of them now. But they didn't do her any good. Inside a few seconds Hal had her right wrist twisted behind her back. She could not budge without breaking that wrist.

But they hadn't been watching Pretty.

There didn't seem to be any reason why they should watch Pretty. He was sick. He was delirious. He didn't amount to much. Not in that sort of condition.

The shouting had aroused Pretty. He sat up on his mattress. In a distant way, he knew something was wrong. They were all bawling at each other. Pretty swayed on to his feet. He wanted to go over to them. To find what it was about. He tried to reach them. His feet wouldn't keep a straight course. He couldn't even see them properly. They were a vague blur.

He bumped against the pressure stove. It rolled over gently, making little noise. And the floor started to burn.

This floor was dry. And it was old. The flames ran fast along the boards. They had a firm hold when Ivan saw them. He saw Pretty, too. Pretty was still trying to reel towards them.

Ivan gave out an oath.

He bunched his right fist and he gave it to Pretty on his broken jaw. Pretty folded like a pocketknife. Ivan bawled at Hal.

'Let go that dame. We gotta get this out.'

They tried to stamp out the flames. It was hopeless. And the shack was filling with smoke. It'd be burned out in a few more minutes.

While Ivan and Hal were concentrating on the flames, Tina started to move towards the door. Tearle watched her for a moment. Then he followed. They reached the door okay. Tearle was opening it when Ivan saw them.

Ivan grabbed in his pocket for his gun. He got it out.

But the place was too full of smoke for him to see properly. He could not even attempt to aim.

Tearle pushed Tina into the clean air of the night. She was coughing and so was he. He got outside himself and slammed shut the heavy door. There was a length of wood on the ground. It looked like it had been the handle of a spade. Tearle picked it up and rammed it through the door handle so that one end of it was pressed against the wall. Now the door could not be opened from the inside. Ivan and Hal would have to get out through the window.

And that would take time. Time enough for them to get clear.

The car that had been Cullen's was nearest. Tearle pushed Tina into it. As he did so, he thought; 'What the devil are you doing this for? You should've lifted this witch back in the shack and let her roast.'

He was about to start up the engine when Tina touched his arm.

'Wait,' she breathed urgently. 'I wanta make sure of something.'

She got out. Tearle watched her run back to the shack. The roof of the place was alight now. She went to where the single set of windows were. There was a thick wood shutter outside them. She started to drag that shutter across the panes.

Through the glass, Ivan's head could be seen. It was swathed in smoke, like it was floating in a cloud. Then he broke the glass and it shattered outwards. But he hadn't time to get through. Tina slammed the hinged shutters over his face and dropped the bar across them.

Inside, his voice could be heard. And Hal's, too. The words could not be made out and they were mixed with the sound of violent coughing.

Tearle pressed the starter, got into gear,

and rolled slowly down the rough track.

After a short while Tina said: 'Just where are we going?'

She said it smoothly, almost casually.

'Where d'yer think? To the law. To Vallis City. Even those cops'll have to hold you now.'

She started breathing heavily. She ran a hand over her smoke-streaked face.

'You ain't. We've got different plans ahead of us. I ain't gonna be handed over to the cops like a trussed bird . . . '

She suddenly leaned forward. Her hand left her face and closed over the ignition key. She turned off the engine and threw the key out of the side window.

13

Tina Departs

That key was lost for good. Tearle knew that before he skidded to a stop. It was hopeless to look for it in the dark, but even if it had been daylight it would have been impossible to find it. On the side of the track where the key had gone out there was a rocky drop of four hundred feet. It would be resting in the valley below. But Tearle wasn't worrying a lot about that. There's an easy way of fixing a car so it'll start without an ignition key.

He said to Tina: 'This isn't getting you anywhere, sister.'

She was watching him with a queer intensity. 'I wanta talk with you. There are a whole lot of things we've gotta get sorted out.'

Tearle didn't answer. He waited for her to go on talking. It was like waiting for a burst of gunfire. Tina was like that. There could be danger in her words.

She said: 'We can still go places. Sure — the law'll be after us but we can be smarter than the law. We can get dough to get started again. I can get the dough. It's always easy for me.'

Tearle said: 'I can believe that, sister. But you know what? Daks was a wholesome citizen compared with you.'

She stiffened slightly. She was going to say something.

Or do something, maybe. But there was a sudden interference. It came from far away.

A red glow began to fill the car. Tearle looked out of the back window. In the distance the burning shack could be seen. The flames were at their zenith, licking towards the sky.

Tina started laughing. A soft and mad laugh. It went on for quite a time.

Tearle started to feel behind the dashboard. He was groping for the electric leads to the ignition switch. He found them, pulled them free then joined the ends together. The warning light went on. The engine was ready to go.

Before he started it, he said: 'You might as well enjoy your laugh now, sister. Your own turn to roast won't be so far off. Only you'll do it formally — in a high voltage chair.'

The car had good headlights. He was able to take the speed past the seventy mark without a lot of danger on the deserted road. Anyway, without a lot of danger until Tina got busy.

She gave no sort of warning. In one second she was slumped in that seat, looking like she was beaten, done. In the next she was wrenching at the driving wheel. At the sort of speed they were moving at, you don't need much of a wrench to take a car off the road. That was just what almost happened.

The car veered over to the far side as Tina twisted savagely at the rim. Tearle let out a curse. With one hell of an effort he pulled it back. Now the auto began swerving in the opposite direction. There were thick woods on either side of that road. They could mean sudden death.

His hand went out to switch off the engine. Then he remembered.

He couldn't switch off the engine. There was no key. The terminals were joined behind the dash.

To brake suddenly would put them into a skid. But it could be done slowly. He shifted his right foot over to the brake pedal. And at the same moment Tina pushed out her shoe and pressed the accelerator flat on the floor.

The engine picked up to a high whine and the speed indicator flickered up to near ninety.

But Tina hadn't finished yet. She was leaning half across Tearle so obscuring his vision. Then the headlights went out. He was hardly able to see at all. Tina had pushed over the switch.

He was lucky. This strip of road was straight. Somehow he held the car as he kicked her right ankle. It came away from the gas pedal. The car began to slow . . .

* * *

The Federal patrols had been out since early that afternoon. Ten radio cars had fanned out along the roads out of Vallis

City. Those boys had started with a whole lot of enthusiasm. This assignment was a State Governor's order. That made it kind of important. But the enthusiasm didn't last so long. Not when after six hours there was no trace of the mob.

It was figured that the mob must have taken to a hideout somewhere near the city. As it got dark they concentrated the search on areas inside of fifty miles of Vallis.

There were false leads, of course. You always get plenty of those. So there wasn't a lot of optimism when some folks in a small town reported a fire in the direction of a disused prospector's shack. The mob weren't likely to draw attention to themselves by setting places alight. But it had to be investigated. A patrol car was detailed off for the job.

It was getting near the locality when they saw a car ahead of them. It was stopping. And its lights were turned off.

★　★　★

Tearle said: 'I'm gonna fix you so you won't be able to twitch an eyebrow.'

173

But Tina held him off. Both her hands were extended and pressing against his chest.

'It ain't no good,' she breathed. 'You can't fix me. No one can. I ain't gonna be handed over to the law. It would have been best if we'd both gone together in this car — the way I tried to fix it. But you were too smart honey. You're a smart guy. But not smart enough to deliver me . . .'

A car was coming up the road towards them. The headlights suddenly bathed them in light. Both watched, rigid, as it braked opposite them.

Tina swore. Then she said: 'It's a Federal patrol.'

She moved fast. She had the door open before Tearle could do a thing about it.

She whispered in a broken kind of way: 'So long, honey . . .'

Then she rushed towards the forest. A few moments later she had disappeared among the trees. Tearle stayed where he was behind the wheel. Somehow he didn't want to go after her now. The law was here. The law had the job to do.

A face was pushed into the car. The face said: 'Get out. We want to talk to you.'

Wearily, he did what they ordered. The Feds gathered round.

A new face pushed its way to the front. Tearle was only faintly aware of it. Only dimly realised who it was. But he felt a little better when this man put a hand around his shoulder and said: 'You're okay, bud. It sure was tough work, but I got to see the governor and he listened.'

It was Dugan. Tearle wanted to say something to him.

Wanted to thank him, maybe. But he couldn't. Right now, he just felt like sleeping. Sleeping for days.

Dugan pushed something into his hand. It was a flask.

Tearle pulled on it deep. Some of the clouds were pushed out of his head. He could talk now.

He said: 'You sure got in for the kill.'

Dugan grinned.

'Yeah and it was easy. The Feds wanted me with them. They figured I might be a help.'

A Fed in a white panama asked: 'And your identity, buddy?'

Dugan answered for him. The Fed's attitude changed.

He said: 'Your friend can look after you, just to see you don't come to any harm. We'll go and fetch the dame. She won't be hard to find.'

The Feds moved into the trees. Dugan gave Tearle a cigarette. They stood on the road. Smoking. Not talking. If they were doing anything important, it was listening. Listening for some indication of what was happening among the tall redwoods.

They did not have to wait for so long. Not more than a few minutes. But it seemed a whole lot longer.

First, they heard the Feds shouting.

And Tina came out of the trees and stood still on the highway.

She was about forty yards from the cars. Her dress was torn. She'd lost one of her shoes. Some of her hair was hanging over her face.

Tina started to run towards them, kicking off the other shoe so as to be able to move faster. The search party came out of the forest a little way behind her.

A little to the rear of Tearle and Dugan there was the sound of rustling undergrowth. A single Federal man came out on to the road, placing himself in front of Tina. This Fed pulled out his gun.

'Okay, ma'am,' he said. 'You can relax now. This is the pay-off.'

She stood opposite him, eyes staring and breathing like the process gave her pain.

Then she grabbed for his gun. It was a mad, wild grab. The Fed moved his arm, but not quickly enough. She had her thumb over his trigger finger. The barrel was aimed right at her. And she was forcing the trigger back.

The Fed realised what she was trying to do. But he realised it too late. As he made up his mind to twist the barrel away from her, the firing pin was released.

The bullet went through her neck.